Landscaping & Leasing

Indie Sparks

Twice Shy Publishing

Print ISBN: 979-8-9894780-4-0

Author's Note

I don't have a single ex with whom I'd want a second chance. I've never advised a friend to get back with an ex, either.

Then again, none of us ever got ghosted by Declan Chillicothe. Or had him walk back into our life five years later, trying to be all nice and professional while looking like sugar-coated sin and talking in that panty-melting voice of his. And then inviting us to lunch and offering answers to the questions that have haunted us for the past five years.

Apologizing.

How dare he?

Of course, if Carina had refused him, none of us would ever know what might have been. And I just couldn't leave us hanging like that.

Welcome back to The Nouveau!

Content Disclosure

This book is intended for mature readers as it contains explicit intimate scenes, profanity in dialogue, and the consumption of alcohol. All characters are consenting adults.

There are scenes that portray a strained relationship between an adult child and her parents. The heroine's mother is an Emily Gilmore type, especially meddlesome and critical. Dialogue during intimate scenes includes raw language and at least one instance of mild degradation. If these factors may be triggering for your wellbeing, please proceed with care when choosing whether to read.

Entertainment is the sole purpose of this story. It should in no way be construed as factual or instructional.

Carina

I speak without looking up because I need to finish typing this email. If I could finish one thing today without being interrupted . . . "Be with you in just a moment."

"Please, take your time. I'm a little early. Traffic was light." His voice sparks embers at the base of my spine.

No, it can't be.

Please let me be having some sort of neurological episode. An auditory hallucination, maybe? Anything would be preferable to him actually being here.

My eyes cautiously drift from my computer screen toward the man whose voice has caused the tremor in my core. "Declan Chillicothe. You own Rough Hands Landscaping?"

"Guilty."

"I didn't accuse you of anything. Yet." My tone has shifted from casual to caustic. Five minutes ago, I'd have sworn I had no anger left for him, but fuck if I don't want to hurl a stapler at his gorgeous face right now.

He's not smiling, just giving me that look—the one that says he's up for a challenge, eager to see my next move. "Hi."

"Did you know it was going to be me?"

"I had a hunch when my office manager told me I was meeting with a woman named Carina."

"I wish I'd confirmed your name." From now on, I'm looking up the owners of every potential vendor before we agree to do business with them.

"Can I take you to lunch?"

"I already hired your company, Dec. No need to schmooze me to get my business."

"I always like to swing by and meet new customers after the first time my crews come out." He has a seat in one of the two chairs on the other side of my desk, makes himself comfortable. "So, how'd we do?"

"You have eyes. Feel free to walk the grounds and see for yourself."

"I'll do that before I leave, but as the customer, what is your impression of the job we did?"

"Your prices are a little steep." I definitely should've hired Vaughn's guy. Our maintenance supervisor knows a vendor for everything, but his landscaping guy gave me a bad vibe. When the foreman for Rough Hands Landscaping walked in the next day with a business card and a price sheet, I hired them on the spot.

We were in a bind. I made a snap decision. And now I'm staring at the biggest mistake of my life . . . one my body might like to make again. How can he still have this instant effect on me?

Sorcery. It's the only logical answer.

"We do good work, and I pay my guys a fair wage. We're fully insured and have well-maintained, reliable equipment. Everything comes at a cost, but I like to think the quality of our service is worth it."

In my head, I'm mimicking him: *but I like to think the quality of our service . . ."*

He tilts his head and narrows his hazel eyes, as if he can hear my mocking thoughts. The sight of his jawline could still give a sketch artist an orgasm. But I'm not a sketch artist.

At best, it has my panties a little wet. Okay, maybe my pussy has clenched a few times, but that means nothing. And my nipples were hard long before he walked in. My manager, Landry, set the air conditioner to arctic blast this morning, and I keep forgetting to turn it down.

Or up, I mean. I think. Fuck. Whatever.

How am I supposed to know up from down with my greatest heartbreak sitting across from me, radiating all his villainous sex appeal, wielding that shit like a weapon?

"As far as I can tell, your guys did a good job. They showed up on time, so that's a plus. Hell, the fact y'all showed up at all is damn plus." I exhale through laughter. I'm no good at the tough girl act, and Declan always saw right through me, anyway. But did I have to melt in under five minutes? I want to be an ice queen in his presence, not a damn puddle.

"Yeah, I keep hearing that from customers. I'd like to stand out for more than the bare minimum, but it seems my competition is setting the bar low these days." His eyebrows lift as if he intended some double entendre, like he's asking an unspoken question.

If he thinks I'm going to give away anything about my current personal life, he's delusional. "Well, so far, you're ahead of the rest."

Oh, give me a break with that smug smile.

He knows I didn't mean him personally. "Your company, that is."

Never hurts to clarify in moments like this.

With a man like him.

"Good to know."

Landry breezes back in from her lunch break, carrying shopping bags. I wonder why she didn't take them up to her apartment.

"I got you a pre-sent," she sing-songs, still lost in her post-shopping happy place, completely unaware of Declan's long legs, spread out in front of my desk like he lives here.

She has the sex toy halfway revealed when she finally spots him and drops it back into the depths of the bag. I don't have to see the other half to know my present is a two-part toy: a clit sucker on one end and a thruster on the other.

We talked about them all morning, and we might've watched a few videos, just to be sure we fully understood how they worked. But I never dreamed she was going to buy me one on her lunch break!

I upset Landry first thing this morning by telling her I abandoned all dating sites over the weekend. I've *given up on love,* as she put it. She said if I wasn't going to try to land a real boyfriend, I at least needed the top-of-the-line rechargeable model. That was the comment that sent us down the deluxe-dildo rabbit hole to begin with.

Now, I apparently own one.

And my ex saw it for the first time right along with me.

"I didn't realize you were going shopping," I say.

Her smile is part apology, part intrigue. "Hi," she says, extending her hand to Declan.

I intervene to complete the introductions. "This is our manager, Landry. Landry, this is Declan. He owns the new landscaping company I hired last week."

"It's so nice to have a company that shows up when they're scheduled. And I can't remember the last time an owner followed up in person," she gushes. "You're blowing your competition out of the water."

He glances at the bag in her hand. "I sure hope so."

They both laugh like that's the funniest thing they've ever heard, like it's not at all weird that my manager bought me a sex toy. To be fair, she's way more than my manager at this point. We've become close friends, but damn, sometimes, she really needs to read the room. Landry has two modes: all business and all play. There is no midrange.

Declan's laughter fades, and he studies me more seriously. "Wait, you're not the manager?"

"Not here. I'm a leasing agent."

"Oh, I assumed—"

Landry cuts him off. "She'll be the assistant manager next week after the new leasing agent starts."

Declan still looks confused, and why wouldn't he?

"I didn't mean there was anything wrong with being a leasing agent. It's just that you were the manager when I knew you, so . . ." He trails off.

"Yeah, I was. Different time, different place."

Landry knows the story, and I can see the lights going off behind her eyes while she makes the connection.

"Let me take you to lunch, Carina." There's a pleading in his voice, but I'm not falling prey to it.

"Vendors take managers to lunch, not leasing agents."

"I've already been to lunch," Landry says. "You should go. Catch up."

If I could shoot lasers from my eyes, she'd be a pile of ash. I want to grab that dual-purpose pleasure device and hit her upside the head with both ends of it. "I brought my lunch."

"Eat it tomorrow," they say at the same time. Great, they've known each other for less than five minutes, and they've already formed an alliance.

"No, I'm not going to lunch with you," I say with conviction. "Your company is doing great so far. Keep up the good work." I turn back to my computer.

Declan stands, and his shadow falls across my desk like it's reaching for me. "I know you weren't expecting me to walk back into your life like this," he says. "Or any way at all, but it's good to see you. Let me know if you need anything from Rough Hands."

I don't have to see Landry's face to know her eyes flew wide at that comment. She doesn't know the name of the landscaping company. And then she confirms it with a faint, "Ohhhhh, damn."

Real subtle, Landry.

"Rough Hands Landscaping," I say without turning around. "It's the name of his company."

Declan pauses at the door to laugh, and I drop my head to keep myself from stealing one last glance at him before he leaves.

Declan

I THOUGHT I WAS prepared to see her. I wasn't. Not even fucking close. One look into those big amber eyes and my knees were ready to hit the carpet. And my mouth was ready to beg for forgiveness—not just with words, either.

She hates me, and she has every right. It wasn't her fault I lost my job back then. That was on my uncle for being such a damn coward that he let other people dictate how he ran his business.

One good thing came out of it: I never forget to run my business on my own terms, nobody else's. It's served me well so far. But that's no consolation for losing Carina.

Fuck, who am I kidding? I didn't *lose* her. I ghosted her.

There is no necessary reason for me to go back to The Nouveau to see her again. I've done my customary meet and greet with management. Why didn't I try harder to convince her to go to lunch with me?

Her manager was on my side, but I just let it go. I had this plan in my head about how we'd go to lunch, and I'd explain everything. She'd forgive me, and we'd start over again with fresh perspectives. If there was no spark between us anymore, we'd at least become friends. Cordial business associates, at worst.

I didn't meet with maintenance. They're usually the ones who call if there's a problem, so I really should have asked Carina if their guys were available while I was there.

"Pick a lane, asshole!" Gotta love Houston traffic. The driver flips me off, and I return the gesture. "Get off your phone and drive!" He speeds ahead, whipping between an eighteen-wheeler and a pickup truck. Fucking idiot.

Darwinism waiting to happen on I-10. Must be a day that ends with a Y.

"Call Carina," I say, trying to speak clearly, but I'm sure I said it too fast. I'm still getting used to giving verbal commands to my phone. I never pick it up to make a call while I'm driving, but it's getting harder to wait until I can pull over to check messages or return a call. And yes, I still have her number in my contacts.

The feminine robot voice replies, "No listing found in contacts for the arena."

"I didn't ask you to call an arena. I said, Call Cuh Ree Na."

"No listing found in contacts for Curry Nah."

"Caa Ree Nuh!"

"No listing found in contacts for Carrie Nun."

"You piece of shit!"

"No listing found in contacts for Hugh P. Sufchit."

"Goddammit!" I floor it and pass the car next to me so I can whip over to the exit lane. My truck jumps the curb, and I yank the wheel to keep from slamming into a concrete planter full of half-dead agave as I pump the brakes in the gas station parking lot.

It was a journey from the freeway to this spot, but one I clearly had to take.

I grab my phone and use it the old-fashioned way. Her voicemail picks up. Fine. Whatever. "Hey, Rina, it's Dec. I totally forgot to ask if your maintenance staff was available while I was there. Give me a shout and let me know when I can set up a time to meet with them. All right. Talk to you soon. Bye."

Aw, shit. Maybe I shouldn't have used that nickname for her. That was way too casual. Way too familiar, which we're not anymore. That will probably piss her off even more. I'm on a roll today.

The smell of fast-food fries wafts in through the air vents. Yeah, food, that's what I need.

I ease into the adjoining Whataburger parking lot and angle into the drive-thru line. The office calls. "Hey, Tess. What's up?"

"Did you already go by The Nouveau?"

"Yeah, just left a little while ago. I'm grabbing some lunch."

"Not fast food, right?"

This is what I get for asking my office manager to ride my ass about eating healthy. She actually does it. "I'm in a hurry today. No choice. Why'd you ask about The Nouveau?"

"We overcharged them and I was—"

"Oh, come on! Of all the fucking properties to screw up the billing on, it had to be that one?"

"It's not like we didn't charge the right amount. We just didn't apply their new client discount on their first service. I was going to have you ask the manager if they wanted me to send a corrected invoice or put a credit on their account. That's all. Geez. You're hangry."

"That's why I'm trying to eat. Just put a credit on their account."

"Do you want to reach out to them and ask what they'd prefer? It might make a better impression if you acknowledge—"

"No. I already left one message there this afternoon."

"I thought you said you just left the property."

"Apply the credit. I'm pulling up to the speaker. Gotta go." I end the call before she can argue.

"Give me a double-meat Whataburger with cheese, no onions, large fries, and a large half-sweet tea."

"That's a double-meat Whataburger, no cheese, just onions, large fries, and a large sweet tea?"

It's going to be one of those afternoons. "No." I sigh and repeat my order. Two more tries and I think they've finally got it right. Time will tell.

I park at the H-E-B across the street to eat. The grocery store parking lot is usually good for people watching. Last time I sat here to eat my lunch, I saw a guy walking out with a live parrot on his shoulder, and a woman, who had to be at least eighty, wearing her long gray hair in pigtails, a sequined crop top, cut-off shorts, and cowboy boots walking in. When their paths crossed, they just nodded at each other and kept walking.

The best kind of people: the ones who mind their own damn business.

An incoming call lights up my phone. I don't recognize the number, but I roll down my window, spit out a piece of onion, and answer it, anyway. "This is Declan Chillicothe."

"Hey, Declan. This is Vaughn Sawyer. I'm the maintenance supervisor at The Nouveau. Carina asked me to call you about coming out, but I think we're good. Your guys showed up and got the job done."

"Thanks for getting back to me. I was in the office earlier, but I didn't think to ask about meeting you. It's been a day. Any chance I could come by later in the week and introduce myself?"

His silence speaks volumes. He hates this shit. Truth be told, I don't love it either, but he probably has his own preferred landscaping company he'd rather use, and that's exactly why I need to meet him in person. It never hurts to put a face to the name, and contrary to the way I'm handling them this afternoon, I'm usually good with people.

"Yeah, sure. How about Friday afternoon sometime? I'll be around until about five."

"Friday works. I look forward to meeting you, Vaughn."

"Likewise."

He's lying, but that's okay. It won't make any difference to him whether I show up to meet him on Friday or not. I think I might like this guy already. Unless I find out he's seeing Carina. Then I'll have to turn him into mulch.

The way she'd want to kick my ass for that thought puts a smile on my face. My lunch order is about as wrong as it could be, but I can't even be mad about it. I've got another reason to show up at her property, and all I can feel is an old weakness coming on strong.

Carina

LANDRY MAKES IT ALMOST to the end of the day before she can't resist any longer. "Okay, are we going to talk about him or what?"

"Who?"

"Oh, do not even try that. You know who. Mr. Rough Hands."

A swish of neon yellow fabric catches my eye, and I know before my vision even focuses that it's one of The Nouveau's remaining original two residents, Vonnie—aka Vonita Viper back in her burlesque days—and her snake, Lolita. The bright red and orange diamond pattern of Lolita's skin against her owner's striking yellow caftan sharpens as they enter the office.

"What's an old broad got to do to get a glass of vino around here?"

"Coming up, Vonnie." She loves to show up around closing time to sip on the boxed wine we keep in the fridge and gossip, which I normally love, but not when I'm about to be the subject of the gossip.

Landry's smile is victorious, knowing she has an ally before she even begins. "You have excellent timing today, Vonnie."

"What do you mean today? Honey, my timing's been good since before you were born." She rubs her snake's head on her cheek, and Lolita's forked tongue darts out.

I pour three glasses of wine. The desire to slam the first two is strong, but unlike Landry, who lives onsite, I have to drive home. Guzzling full glasses of wine isn't a habit of mine, but right now, I'm theoretically up for anything that could dull my senses before this conversation gets too deep.

In reality, I'll remain sober and take the hits to my dignity. This has been a very unfair day overall.

Nothing has been fair where Declan is concerned since the day my parents fired his uncle's landscaping company because he was dating me. Such a bizarre truth, and explaining it to other people only highlights the fuckery of it all. But here we go again.

"Let happy hour commence!" I pass out the wine glasses, and then I lock the office door. Vaughn walks past and looks in to see if Landry is leaving yet. He shakes his head and smiles when he sees her lifting her glass with Vonnie. I smile back at him and shrug.

He'll have to go upstairs alone, but I know he'll listen for her door across the hall, and neither one of them will remain alone for long.

Ever since they stood up to my parents and said they'd quit their jobs before they'd stop seeing each other, they've been our resident power couple.

"Get over here and start spilling your secrets, girl," Vonnie says with a laugh. She is a woman who has no secrets, the walking definition of an open book.

"It was more of an accident than a secret." I take my first sip of wine. "I accidentally hired an ex's company to do our landscaping."

"And?"

"And he stopped by to introduce himself this afternoon." I take a much larger sip of wine. "Which was total bullshit because he knew he was coming to meet me, but I was completely unprepared to see him. He blindsided me! On purpose!" My voice is rising, and my grip is tightening on my glass.

"Sounds like he had reason to believe you wouldn't have wanted to see him." Vonnie eyes me over the rim of her glass, her dyed red curls falling forward to frame her face.

Landry laughs. "Listen, there's not a woman alive who wouldn't have wanted to see that man." She looks at me and grins. "Sorry, but you know it's true. Did he always look like that?"

"Yes," I admit with a defeated sigh. "He's always been hot. And he's aging way too damn well."

"Oh, good-looking men always age well," Vonnie says. "For a while, anyway. It'll catch up to him someday."

"When is it going to catch up to you?" I tease. She's the youngest looking seventy-something-year-old woman alive.

"My attitude keeps me young. That and walking every day, drinking a few glasses of wine every night, and taking care of my Lollie Girl." She nuzzles the snake.

Landry's eyes meet mine, and we share a quick, knowing glance. She swears she saw Vonnie leaving a sex club with our other original resident, Autry McDaniel. If she's right, I think our favorite tenant's extracurriculars with her buttoned-up-widower neighbor might be a factor in keeping her young, too. But of course, I keep that to myself. Honestly, the woman is an inspiration.

"And a little dirty fun time with a man now and then doesn't hurt either," Vonnie waggles her perfectly filled-in eyebrows. "The day I'm too old and weak to entertain a hard dick, just toss me in a hole and throw dirt on me."

Landry chokes on her wine. Vonnie still shocks her sometimes. I've been around her for too long, but she still makes me laugh.

"Good for you, Vonnie." I give her a wink. "Get that D."

We clink our glasses together, but she narrows her eyes at me. "What about you, honey? How much D are you getting these days?"

"I'm doing fine in that department."

"No, she's not," Landry counters.

"Well then, sounds like your ex may have shown back up at the perfect time."

Landry nods. "I think he did."

"Shit!" I set my glass on my desk and look at my phone. "I was supposed to go to yoga tonight, and I totally forgot about it."

"Uh-oh," Vonnie says. "You missed your workout. Maybe you better call that ex and see if he can help you work out instead."

"I won't be calling Declan to help me do anything."

"Oh, that's a good name." Vonnie repeats it. "Declan. You don't hear that one often. It's manly. I like it."

"It fits him, too," Landry says.

"You can both stop. There will be no rekindling between Declan and me. But since I'm not going to yoga anyway, who needs a refill?"

Being alone doesn't normally make me feel lonely. I have an active social life, and I appreciate my alone time. Usually. Tonight, my apartment feels strange. The energy is weird. Tense.

I wash the new toy Landry gave me because I've got to break it in at some point. I've been curious since we watched those videos, and now I own one, so I may as well use it.

Leaving the device to dry on my bathroom counter, I pour myself a fresh glass of wine. The two I had in the office did nothing to take the edge off my nerves.

A few episodes of reality TV are over in the blink of an eye, and my glass is empty again. I could've done something healthier, like meditate or go for a walk, but I needed to wallow a bit. Some forgotten feelings are punching me in the heart, old memories confusing my head. I just needed to throw myself a small pity party.

My new rechargeable boyfriend is nearly dry. I pat the remaining moisture with a towel and take it to bed with me. It's fully charged, but there's no way I'll get through all these settings: ten thrusting options, ten vibration frequencies, and ten *biting sensation modes*? Holy shit. The booklet says it's softer than a human mouth, making the options all pleasurable.

We'll see about that.

I coat the curved-tip thruster with lube and push it inside my pussy, testing a few settings until I find one with the right timing. *Damn, that's nice.* I tug lightly on the cord that connects the two parts of the toy, and my walls clench around the thruster.

Kicking the covers down to my thighs to give myself more room for testing the exterior component, I gently set it against my labia and adjust the settings. My hips jerk a little when I test out the supposed biting simulation.

I explore a few more modes and settle on one that feels like it's alternating licks and nibbles. And people are excited about self-driving cars? This is the witchcraft we need right here.

My spine softens against the mattress as I move the fake flower-mouth over my tender skin, letting the top of it barely graze my clit. Once my body adjusts to the sensations, my eyes drift closed. It takes no effort at all to imagine a man's mouth in place of the toy.

His mouth. I shouldn't want it to be him, but secret facts are what they are.

I glide the toy upward to fully enclose my clit. The surface is large enough that it's still massaging my folds while it sucks on my clit, and the thruster is teasing over my G-Spot, but it's his fingers there, just like it's his mouth on my clit and his phantom rough hands roaming over the rest of my body.

The gentle tingling in my core heats up as it spreads lower. My clit swells, making the sucking sensation feel stronger, and my pussy spasms and my back arches and my thighs and ass quake and his voice is in my ear—the vibration of his words tickling my eardrum as if he's everywhere all at once . . . and it's his name on my lips when I come.

Welcome back to my fantasies, Dec. You gorgeous fucking asshole.

Declan

I COULD KNOCK OFF early today and get home before the Friday rush hour traffic starts, but I'm supposed to meet the maintenance guy at The Nouveau. No way I'm skipping that.

There's an open parking spot next to the curb near the office. I send Vaughn a text to let him know I'm here and wait all of five seconds for a reply before I decide to go into the office. The Nouveau is a tower, so it's not likely I'd find him if I walked around the grounds, and I don't have access to the garage. What choice do I have?

Her eyes flit away as soon as she sees me.

"Got any idea where I can find your maintenance supervisor? I'm supposed to meet him this afternoon."

The manager answers my question. "I think he's changing the pool filter."

A man too young to be the one I'm looking for comes around the corner wearing a shirt that says maintenance over the chest pocket. "Actually, I just took care of that. You looking for Vaughn?"

"I am."

"Is he expecting you?"

"He is." Who the hell is this kid? He's awfully protective of his boss.

"He's upstairs in the supply room. I'll take you up there."

"Thanks." I look back at Carina, but she won't even give me a half-glance. "Good to see you again, Rina." She gives me no reaction at all, but I didn't expect her to. She's as stubborn as ever.

As I walk out of the office, I hear her manager say, "Aw, he calls you Rina?"

The young man leading me to the elevator sticks out his hand. "Hey, I'm Holden."

"Declan. Nice to meet you." Holden seems awfully proud to be taking me up to meet Vaughn. "Is he your dad?"

"Vaughn?" The kid cracks up. "Holy shit, dude. Don't tell him you asked me that."

"So, I guess that's a no."

"It's a hard no. I mean, he'd probably make a decent dad. He's got a dad attitude, that's for sure, but he's not old enough to be my dad. He's like, your age."

"Oh, okay. I wasn't sure."

"It's all good. I'd be pissed if my dad was dating Landry. At least if I had to lose out to a guy, he's not as old as my dad."

"Your maintenance supervisor and your manager are dating?"

"Yeah. They used to try to keep it a secret, but they finally gave up and just started being a couple out in the open."

"It's understandable why they'd want to keep it a secret in the beginning. Workplace relationships can get complicated." *More complicated than you can imagine sometimes.*

The moment I meet Vaughn, I know him. We've never met, but I know this guy. And I can totally see him and the manager together. His girlfriend seems to like me well enough; maybe if he and I hit it off, I'll have two of Carina's coworkers on my side.

"Hey, sorry," he says. "I just saw your text."

"No worries. Holden came along at the perfect time."

"Yeah, he has a habit of doing that." Vaughn eyes the kid, and I can't tell for sure if he likes him or not. "If you got that pool filter changed, you can take off."

"Cool. See you Monday."

"Good luck this weekend."

"Thanks, man." Holden walks out wearing the biggest smile his face can hold.

"There's gotta be a date involved if wishing him good luck makes him smile like that."

Vaughn shakes his head. "He's a film major, and he's got something in a competition at some festival."

"Ah, that's a world I can't pretend to know anything about."

"Me either, but I think he might be pretty good at it. You want a beer?"

"Yeah, sure."

He jerks his head to indicate I should follow him. We stop in front of an apartment, and before he opens the door, he glances at the one directly across the hall.

"She was still downstairs when I came in," I say.

Vaughn laughs. "No secrets around here, I guess."

He opens the door, and I follow him inside. I knew this was a nice property, but if they include this apartment in his benefits, he hit the fucking lotto. "Nice place."

"Yeah, one of the reasons I took the job. Used to swear I'd never live in this part of town, but it grows on you."

"Only if you can afford to live here."

"You want to go up to the roof?"

There's a cool breeze, and he buys good beer. Nothing to fault so far. He unfolds a couple of camp chairs and provides buckets to put our feet on. I've definitely met new clients under worse conditions.

Vaughn's a pretty easy guy to like. We talk about our backgrounds, how we both ended up in the business. I avoid talking about Carina . . . until he does.

"So, you're the guy, huh?"

"I can't commit to that without more information."

"With Carina. The one her parents made the non-fraternization policy for?"

"I was the reason for that policy?"

"You didn't know that?"

"No. She told me they didn't want us seeing each other, but I thought the policy was already in place. I thought we were breaking an existing rule, not one that was created just for us."

"Shit, man. I'm sorry. Her parents are something else, her mom in particular."

"Yeah, they leave a hell of an impression." I tip my beer back, trying not to let the extent of my shock show. *It was specifically for me? They were so sure I'd be that bad for their daughter? I never even met those people. They didn't know shit about me!*

"Your guys do good work."

"Let me know if they ever don't." I sink my empty bottle back into his ice chest and stand up. "Thanks for the beer. It was a pleasure to put a name to the face. Call me if you need anything."

"Will do. Hunt me down and say hi when you're onsite."

"Yeah, I'll have to get you out of here for lunch one day."

"I'll take you up on it."

He stands, but I put my hand up. "Keep enjoying your spot. I can find my way out."

"I've gotta walk you down. You won't get past the elevator without access."

"Right. I forgot about that."

"I'll ride down with you and see if I can convince Landry to come up."

"She'll definitely improve the view more than I did."

We laugh, but I know he can sense my tension. I try to keep up a good front in the elevator, but when we walk to the office, and I see Rina inside, laughing with her manager when *she* should be the fucking manager of a place like this by now, my gut twists. Why isn't she?

I'd know the answer if I hadn't shut her out until it was too late. I knew she wasn't like her parents, but my uncle could've lost his company when he lost his contracts with them. He fired me, but worse, he blamed me. I needed somebody to blame other than myself, so I put it all on her, never knowing it really was all because of me. I was the reason the policy existed to begin with.

And I encouraged her to break it with me. What did she lose because of my selfishness? Probably should've asked myself that question a long time ago. I was still trying to get through college in my mid-twenties because I had to work full-time, feeling behind, like the whole world was passing me by. Tunnel vision. All I could see was my own future, but when the dust settled, I knew I'd fucked up. I just didn't know how to make it right.

It's been five years, and I'm still not sure I know how to make it right.

I might've done more damage than I can repair, but the moment Tess said I was meeting with a woman named Carina, memories I've kept locked away came flooding back. What are the odds she'd still be single? This has all got to mean something. I don't believe in coincidences.

But she doesn't believe in me anymore.

Hoping to catch her attention, I linger for a minute, but she won't look my way, not even when Vaughn opens the door and walks into the office. Landry smiles. Carina looks right past me. Pretends I'm still a ghost.

Carina

I've barely turned my key in the office door when a slithering motion draws my eyes to the side. "Good morning, Lolita. Where's Vonnie?"

"I'm coming!" She whirls around the corner wearing a solid black caftan with leopard print accessories: chunky plastic necklace and matching earrings, the scarf tied in her hair, and sneakers—all leopard. And she's sporting what has got to be the brightest orange lipstick on the market.

"Morning, Vonnie. Are you wearing a new lipstick?"

She purses her lips. "What do you think? Too bright?" Her snake coils around her waist as soon as she scoops her up.

"It's an attention grabber."

"Well, I do like a little attention."

A little. Sure, let's go with that.

"Are you headed out for your morning walk?"

"I'd already be back by now if I hadn't wasted time waiting for that unreliable, insufferable little fedora-wearing prick. At the last minute, he calls to say his allergies are plaguing him, and I should go on without him. I'd have happily gone on without him half an hour ago! Jackass."

"Vonnie, why can't you just admit that you and Autry are friends?" *Especially when you might be so much more than friends.*

"Oh, he's just a fixture in my life because he's been around so damn long. I wouldn't say we're friends."

"It's good to have friends." I step into the office, and she follows. "Even friends with benefits, sometimes." My purse misses my desk when I let it fall from my shoulder, but my chair saves it from hitting the floor. I leave it where it lands and head for the coffeemaker.

"Ha! What benefits could an old coot like him provide?"

You tell me.

"Age is just a number, right?"

"Yeah, yeah, yeah." She plants herself in a chair in front of my desk, making it clear she plans to hang out in the office for a while.

Normally, I wouldn't mind, but our new leasing agent starts today, and I want to get some things done before she shows up. "Weather's nice out there this morning."

"Eh, I'll walk this evening. How's it going with your blast from the past?"

"Declan? There's nothing going on between us. He's just another vendor."

"Sure he is, doll. Well, if you don't have any juicy stories to share, I guess I may as well walk. Come on, Lollie. Let's get some fresh air."

I smile as I watch her go. You just can't help but smile after you've spent a little time with Vonnie.

Landry steps off the elevator, and I watch her interact with Vonnie, shrinking away from Lolita because she's still afraid of snakes. They make such an unlikely pair, chatting and laughing in the lobby: an eccentric older tenant wrapped in a colorful snake, and the office manager in her trendy pale pink wide-legged pants and matching wrap sweater.

Vonnie really didn't like Landry when she first started. She gave her a pretty hard time for a while. Now, she's like her onsite mom. My smile widens.

And then a familiar, tall brunette steps up to them. Well, shit. She's early. Guess I'm not getting anything done before I go into training mode. Vonnie eyes the new leasing agent, and the quirk of her mouth makes it clear she doesn't like her. Uh-oh.

The woman takes instant likes or dislikes to people, and aside from Landry, I've never known her to change her mind. This poor leasing agent could be in for a rough time at The Nouveau. I can tell from Landry's expression she's thinking the same thing.

She walks into the office with our new employee right on her heels. "Good morning, Carina. Molly has already met Vonnie and Lolita, so she's getting to know the VIPs right off the bat." Her mouth smiles, but her eyebrows send up a distress signal.

"Vonnie is one of our two original tenants who still lives here. They've been here since the property opened in 1980." I hope maybe the stats will make an impression.

"She seems like an original, all right." Molly laughs nervously. "Does she always walk around with that snake?"

"Lolita," I say, trying not to let my agitation seep into my voice. I'm protective of Vonnie, and by extension, Lolita. "She used to be a famous burlesque performer, and her stage name was Vonita Viper. Some old ladies have cats. She has a snake."

"At least it's only one snake. It is only one, right?"

"Yes, she just has the one," Landry says. "I'm actually afraid of snakes, but she grows on you. Okay, to be honest, it's Vonnie who's grown on me, but I'm getting better with Lolita."

Molly looks around like perhaps she's made a mistake in taking this job. "Does the other original tenant have any weird pets?"

"No, Autry McDaniel has no pets. He's very proper and businesslike, but he's a sweetheart," Landry says.

"And sometimes he brings us boxes of nearly stale powdered donuts from the grocery store," I add. "Which he offers from the goodness of his heart, and we love them."

"You love cheap powdered donuts?"

"When they come from him, we do," I say, pointedly. Surely, she gets the message. If she needs things explicitly spelled out for her, she's not going to make it here.

"Oh, okay. Got it. Does Vonnie bring any treats I should be aware of?"

Landry laughs. "She's a constant treat."

Vaughn steps in to let us know Holden's out sick. "Hey, I'm Vaughn, the maintenance supervisor. You must be the new leasing agent."

"Yeah, I'm Molly."

"Nice to meet you, Molly."

Her eyes trail him as he walks away. "Damn, speaking of treats."

What the hell is wrong with this woman? That is her boss's boyfriend! I mean, sure, maybe she doesn't know that, but I bet she's about to find out. I wait for Landry's response. *One, two, three—*

"He is indeed." That's all she says.

Seriously? Say more. Go off!

"That'll be your desk," Landry says, pointing to the new one she brought in for her. "But you can pull a chair up to Carina's for the first few days. She'll train you on the software, and you can shadow her if anyone comes in and wants to see an available unit. Your computer won't be here until tomorrow, anyway."

"Great." Molly puts her purse in a drawer of her own desk and rolls her chair next to mine.

I go through the basics of logging on, and then I pull up the tutorial for the software. "I'm going to switch chairs with you and let you go through this on your own first. It's helpful."

Spinning my chair to face Landry, I shoot her a look to convey my doubts about Molly. She responds with a look of her own, one that says I have to give her a chance.

"So, I used your present."

"Oh, yeah? And?"

I let my eyes roll back in my head and flutter my lashes.

She throws up a high-five, I meet her hand with mine.

"I knew I should've gotten myself one."

This is a weird aspect I hadn't considered when we agreed to hire a new leasing agent. All our deeply personal conversations will now have to take place in code, or after work. I guess that's not grounds for firing her, but it's enough to make me wish she wasn't here.

Declan

"Morning, Tess." I drop a bag of gummy worms on her desk. They're her favorites. She appreciates the small things, and I appreciate her. "Can you send some cookies to The Nouveau?"

"Since when do we send cookies to our clients?"

"I'm pretty sure we've done that before."

"I'm positive we haven't."

"Well, we should start. It's good to let customers know you appreciate them."

"And we're starting with The Nouveau? A brand-new customer. Should I address them to Carina or just let that be implied?"

Sometimes, Tess is too perceptive for own good. I turn just in time to see her bite the head off a green gummy worm. "Just send the damn cookies."

Five minutes later, I step out of my office. "Send snickerdoodles."

"I already ordered them. I sent chocolate chip. Everybody loves chocolate chip."

"The Nouveau loves snickerdoodles. Change the order."

"Calling them now, boss." She pops the second half of a red worm into her mouth with a smile. "The Nouveau should certainly have what The Nouveau loves." When she winks, I know she knows. Dammit.

"I'll be out the rest of the day." I grab a stack of business cards from the counter. "How'd you know?"

"The look on your face the moment I said her name. Ex-girlfriend, I assume?"

"Fix the cookie order."

"Should I add some heart-shaped balloons?"

"Eat your worms."

Most days, I think Tess's wife is a lucky woman because of the way Tess picks up on every little detail. Other days, I think it must drive her crazy to be married to a mind reader.

I walk into my chiropractor's office, nod at the receptionist, and hold up my gym bag. She buzzes me back to change into my sweats. It would be easier to wear them on the days I come here, but I don't want Tess to know I'm doing this. She'd want to add my appointments to her own calendar so she could be sure and remind me. I don't need reminders. My lower back reminds me just fine.

It's been six months since the accident, one that I walked away from without a scratch. But not without a residual parting gift. I resisted doing anything about the intermittent pain for several months, but now I come here twice a week. It's helping. Still pisses me off that I have to do it.

My chiropractor is a middle-aged woman named Dorian, who doesn't think I'm funny. Hell, I'm not sure she thinks anything is funny. I still try my sense of humor on her every now and then, but I learned early on not to bullshit her about my back. Honest answers get me better results.

The rest of the world doesn't need to know about it, though. To them, I'm fine. To Dorian, I'm a pain on her patient roster.

I always intend to do the exercises at home, but things come up. And when I go to the gym, I end up overdoing it every time, even when I'm trying to stick to the limits she suggests. I can't help it; if I feel like I can do more, I push myself. It feels weak not to.

I'm long on drive, short on patience.

"I know you think yoga isn't for you," she says as she works on my back. "But I guarantee it would help. What do I know, though? I only have twenty-five years of experience. And it's none of my business if you've got something against a good night's sleep."

"You may be good at your job, but you suck at reverse psychology."

"Will you just humor me and take a flyer from the front desk? It's got a coupon for a free month."

"I don't use coupons."

"Of course, you don't." She makes a final manipulation, and I exhale at the release. "Plenty of men do yoga. Not to mention all the pretty single women."

I laugh. "Yeah, what woman doesn't want a man with a back injury?"

"Your hard head is a bigger turnoff, I'm sure."

"Thanks. I almost left here with my ego unbruised."

"I'd hate to break our routine." She pats my shoulder. "Seriously, you need yoga."

What I need is a cheeseburger. But I'll have something healthier. I'm not entirely self-destructive.

I grab a flyer for the yoga studio on my way out. Whatever. I promised Dorian I'd take one.

Carina

I'VE NEVER NEEDED A yoga class more in my life. What a stressful fucking week. I stand to the side in the lobby of the studio, waiting for the class that's just ended to retrieve their shoes and bags from the cubbies so I can put my stuff in one. I need to get into the practice room early and stretch.

It's not that the new leasing agent, Molly, does anything wrong; she just makes things weird. She's actually picking up on everything quickly, and she's nice. But we had this great family-type vibe going at The Nouveau, and she's like the new step sibling nobody asked for, which is totally unfair to her.

And totally out of character for me. I'm an includer. I draw people in and make them feel welcome. . . why can't I embrace Molly? She's nice. When she found out Landry and Vaughn were a couple, she nearly died of embarrassment over her comment about him being a *treat*.

In all fairness, she deserved to feel ashamed of that. I can't help it. I feel like I feel. But Landry laughed it off, and that was the end of it.

Molly may be nice, but she's nosy. She hasn't asked any questions, but I know she notices when Landry pokes me about Declan. I see her ears perk up.

Those damn cookies he sent didn't help. Snickerdoodles. As if remembering my favorite kind of cookie means anything. He's going to have to try harder than that. Not that I want him to try at all. Or that he is trying. But if he were, it would take more than a warm cookie to sway me.

He hasn't come back around or called to invite me to lunch again. And that's good because I wouldn't go, and I don't need to see him. I don't need Molly to see him either.

Oh, hell. Do I see her as competition?

Why? I'm not even a competitive person. She's not going to take my job. Having her there is enabling me to take on more responsibilities. She's not going to take my friend. Landry has room in her life for more friends, and gaining a new one won't break the bond she has with me. If Molly met Declan and decided he was a *treat*, she'd be free to treat herself to whatever he wanted to offer. I wouldn't care.

I wouldn't.

Fuck. I would so care. Way too much.

Am I . . . the J word? No. No way.

I've worked too hard to reject jealousy in my life. It's a funda-mental part of who I am, a basic tenet of being Carina!

With my flip-flops shoved into a cubby, I cram my purse in on top of them and carry my rolled-up mat and water bottle down the hall.

I'm the third person in the room, so I could easily claim a spot by the windows, which I usually prefer, but tonight, I gravitate to the interior back corner and roll out my mat.

It smells like feet in here. They mop between classes, but I think they may have missed this corner. Is it my mat? I sit up and fold over at the waist, reaching for my toes, and trying to inconspicuously give my mat the sniff test. Nope, it's in the air.

That's a communal funk.

The instructor comes in and lights incense at the front of the room. I wave her over and whisper, "Can you put one back here?"

She takes a whiff and nods. "I'll set one on the shelf."

Stretching feels exceptionally good tonight. I'm glad I got here early.

The instructor brings the promised incense, and she offers me a warm cloth. "I put some eucalyptus oil on it. You can breathe it in to help drown out the smell until the incense has a chance to permeate the air. Plus, it'll give you a little boost."

"Thanks. I could use it tonight."

"I had a feeling." She touches my shoulder reassuringly before she walks away.

This is exactly where I need to be. I spread my legs and crawl my fingertips forward between my feet, inching my nose closer and closer to my mat. I shift my torso to stretch toward my left foot. My spine locks.

What the hell? Is he stalking me?

Declan Chillicothe in a yoga class is not a fucking coincidence. There's no way he's taken up yoga. He doesn't even look remotely comfortable, sitting up straight and stiff on one of the studio's loaner mats while his eyes dart around the room. They land on me, and his mouth falls open.

Look at him, trying to act shocked that I'm here.

He tips his head. "Hey."

Oh, don't you "hey" me.

I mouth a quick "hi," and lower into my full stretch.

Why? Why does he have to ruin this for me? Tonight, of all nights. And who's he trying to impress with no shirt on? He probably heard yoga was a good way to meet women.

Idiot. I hope he pulls a hamstring.

Focusing on my breathing and looking away from the new tattoo on his shoulder is a must if I want to get any benefit out of this class. I hate that I know it's new, but I burned all his old ink into my memory. That skull hugging his deltoid is definitely new. Technically, it could be five years old, but it wasn't there the last time I saw his shoulder, so it's new to me.

Stop staring at it!

The instructor reenters the room and closes the door behind her. Thank goodness. We're about to begin. She fans her hand over the incense to float the scent in my direction as she passes. I inhale.

Zen before men.

We start with sun salutations. This is good. No time for my eyes to wander. I'm fully in my space.

Warrior one. Eyes forward. Strong arms. I got this.

Oh. My. God. He's facing the wrong way.

I watch as it dawns on him. He turns his head. Nope, that's not going to fix it, genius.

You've got the wrong foot forward. You're leading with the wrong arm. Look at your neighbor!

What am I doing, trying to beam him helpful hints? I shake my head. He'll figure it out or he won't. Not my problem. His ineptitude finally catches the instructor's eye, and she comes over to guide him.

Okay, but does she have to put her hands on him like that? Seems excessive. I think a verbal correction would've done the trick.

Why is this the longest yoga class in history? When she takes us through a sequence that shifts our perspectives to the back of the room, an uneasy self-consciousness washes over me. Declan is behind me now. Is he watching me?

A quick glance between my legs in downward dog confirms he's not. Good. He shouldn't be looking at me. I don't want him looking at me.

Can he really not bring his hands any closer to his feet? That's a wide pose. At least he's facing the right direction.

Finally, shavasana.

I know he's got to be hating this. Being still is Declan's least favorite thing in the world, and he probably needs it more than anyone in here.

The instructor quietly tells us to bring motion back to our bodies, moving first our fingers and toes, and then our hands and our feet, our wrists and our ankles. Bodies stir around me, and I sense the shadow of someone standing, even though we haven't been guided into the fetal position, and then on to sitting—we haven't even been told to open our eyes yet.

I know it's an individual practice, but I hate when people rush through this part. I open my own eyes and sit up. The ritual is already ruined.

Declan walks up behind me in the lobby as I'm stepping back into my flip-flops. "I never realized yoga was such a workout."

"Yeah, that's a genuine revelation for some people." I hang my purse on my shoulder and roll my finger to indicate he should follow me.

I lead him to a calendar on the wall and point at the Saturday morning stretching class. "You need this one."

"Do you go to that one, too?"

"Sometimes. But you need to go to it all the time."

"I'd be more inclined to show up if I knew you'd be there."

"Show up. Take your chances. But if you're going to stalk me, you may as well get some much-needed benefits from it." I walk toward the exit.

He follows right behind me. "Stalk you? I didn't come here expecting to find you."

"Really? You just picked this studio at random?"

"No. My chiropractor told me about it. She won't stop nagging me about trying yoga, so I came just so I could say I did."

"Why are you seeing a chiropractor?" I continue across the parking lot, and he stays at my side.

"Because I was in a very minor accident six months ago. I thought I was fine, but I was apparently wrong."

"You've been seeing a chiropractor for six months, and your back is still bothering you?"

"No. More like six weeks."

"That sounds about right." I toss my yoga mat onto my backseat and slam the door. "Ignore the situation until you can't anymore. I see you're as hard-headed as ever."

"My chiropractor would agree with you. Takes one to know one, though." He steps closer. "I assume you got the cookies?"

"Yeah, everyone enjoyed them."

"What about you?"

"Snickerdoodles aren't my favorite anymore."

"I'll send chocolate-chip next time. How about we both go home and shower, and then I take you to dinner? You do still eat dinner, right?"

He's put his shirt back on, but it's a tank top, and I can't stop looking at the skull on his shoulder. It's set against a background of roses, and the artist did a good job. The way my fingertips itch to trace it is obscene. Stupid. "Yeah, but I have food at home."

"I wasn't offering to feed you as an act of charity. I'd really like a chance to explain some things. Please?"

Playing the vulnerability card is a surprise. It works. "Fine. Where do you want to meet?"

"I want to pick you up." I open my mouth to object, but he says, "If I'm driving, you can have as many cocktails as you need to sit through my bullshit."

Dammit. I laugh, and I know he knows he's got me now. "Okay." I give him my address. "Give me an hour."

"I'll be there in forty-five minutes."

"I'll be ready in an hour." And I won't be having any cocktails.

He's right on time—his time, not mine, but I'm ready. I didn't go to any great trouble with my appearance. I'm not trying to impress him. He wants to talk? He can talk to me wearing no makeup and with my hair up in a messy bun.

And I intend to eat a hearty meal, too. Anger makes me hungry.

I told him to text me when he got here, and I'd come down, but he's knocking on my door because he just can't stand to not get his own way. "I said I'd come down."

"But you knew I was going to come up and get you, anyway."

He clearly put a lot more effort into his appearance than I did. And he smells nice, too. He's wasting his time, unless he has big plans with someone else after dinner.

"My favorite look," he says, reaching to touch a stray piece of hair that's fallen across my cheek. He used to always say he loved knowing I was comfortable being real with him.

This was a no-win situation from the start. If I'd gotten all dolled up, he'd have assumed I'd done it for him. I'm all fresh-faced and messy-haired, and he assumes that's for him, too.

"Someone rushed me."

"I never rushed you." He steps into my apartment uninvited, pushing the door closed. I take a step back and consider telling him we should go, that I don't have much time, anything to keep his husky voice from weakening my knees any further. But my voice gets lost, and his deepens. "I always encouraged you to take all the time you needed. Or wanted. Didn't I?"

He takes a giant step, closing the gap between us, but my feet stay rooted in place instead of retreating like my brain is telling them to. My breathing shallows, and my pussy clenches. I know he can only be certain of the former, but the latter is repeating itself, begging for his attention.

"Dec, I, this, it's not—"

His hands cradle my face, his fingers sliding into my hair, loosening more strands. I'm going to have to redo my bun before we go to dinner. We need to go now. Being alone with him, this close to him, it's is a terrible idea. I should put a stop to it.

"Are you going to hate me if I admit how badly I want you right now?" His mouth closes on mine, and my palms go to his chest, intending to pushing him away. But my fingers close to fist his shirt. And I kiss him back. I don't know if I hate him or not, but I absolutely want to fuck him.

"I guess hate fucking could be an option," I whisper against his mouth.

"Whatever you need to tell yourself, beautiful."

He walks me backward into my bedroom, pulling out the hair tie that was holding my bun as we go. Once we're next to my bed, he pulls my shirt off, slides my leggings down until I step out of them, and stares at my body, standing before him in a matching bra and panties—not for his benefit.

I always match. He knows that, but a wolfish grin spreads across his face, anyway. "You always looked good in lace."

"I still wear it for me."

"And that only makes it sexier." He pushes my shoulders, and I topple back onto the bed.

Reaching behind his back, he grabs handfuls of his shirt and pulls it over his head. The detailed skull tattoo appears to cast shadows on his biceps as his muscles work in the lamplight. It's just a trick of the light, but the way it seems to be rolling across his muscle makes me want to touch it all the more. My fingers have mapped all his older ink, but they ache to learn the intricacies of every suture, every sharp-edged opening and tooth . . .

He toes off his shoes, and his jeans hit my floor. His erection bulges in his black boxer briefs, and I know how good it will feel in my hand, but the longing to touch his shoulder and let my hands glide down his muscular arms and his hard abs has my fingers literally twitching at my side.

I slide back toward my headboard, and he climbs onto the bed until he's positioned next to me. Propped on his elbow, leaning over me, he reaches around with one hand and unclasps my bra. He pulls a strap over my shoulder and down my arm so I can slip my hand through, and repeats the action on the other side, baring my breasts. "So beautiful."

The rough pad of his fingertip circles my nipple, and I bite my bottom lip in response. I want him to stop as much as I want him to keep teasing around it all night. My moan when he slides his hand down my ribcage is involuntary. The warmth of his hand spawns a trail of goosebumps, and I jolt when his thumb grazes my hipbone.

His fingers brush the lace top of my panties, tickling over sensitive nerve endings peeking through the scalloped pattern. He traces the path again to watch me shiver beneath him, my nipples hardening further under his gaze.

Just fuck me already. Let's make this mistake and walk into our own regrets tomorrow. Even as I think it, I know he won't pick up the pace. Dec in seduction mode can't be rushed. And he was telling the truth when he said he never rushed me either.

His fingers slip beneath the lace, and he strokes my pussy, which he's probably letting himself believe is freshly smooth, just for him. It's not. I do that for me, too. But the way his fingers feel gliding on my smooth skin steals my breath for a moment.

But it's not just the bare skin enabling the glide.

I'm so fucking wet, and he's spreading my juices everywhere, skirting around my opening to torture me.

"Have you broken in that new toy your boss gave you yet?"

My laughter tumbles between our bodies. "Yes."

"Show me."

"It'll be fast if I do. That thing is a soul snatcher."

"Mmm, I love it when you say snatch." He plunges two fingers inside me, and I gasp. "Is it in your nightstand?"

I nod, wishing he wasn't about to take his fingers away.

He rolls away to open the drawer and lifts the device out, examining it for a few beats before he rolls back to me. "Put it on the setting you like and spread your legs."

It's still too new for me to know my preferred settings yet, so I have to try a few until it feels right in my hand. His eyes watch the thrusting motion I've settled on. "What does the other end do?"

When I tap through the choices for the flower-mouth, his eyebrows lift—part shock, part amusement. "This thing could give a guy a complex."

"Since when are you intimidated by a toy?"

"I usually see them as teammates, but this one might actually be competition."

"It's not. Toys don't have arms or real mouths or a chest for a woman to lay her head on."

"Stroking my ego?"

"Speaking the truth." I lower the toy and set the thruster against my pussy. "Push it inside for me."

His hand closes over mine, his middle finger forcing mine forward. "Deeper?"

"Yeah, a little more."

I move my hand and let him press it farther into me. The opposite end is vibrating in my other hand. When I bring it closer to my body, his eyes follow it.

Touching it to my vulva, I use it to massage up and down, the simulated tongue flicking over my delicate, slick skin while the silicone lips work their magic. It doesn't feel like a real mouth sucking or licking my pussy, but it probably feels as close as anything else could. It's not the same, but it's good.

The thruster is abrading my G-spot with a soft pressure that has my spine undulating. I look up into Dec's eyes and find them glistening with lust. He's fascinated by what he's seeing. So am I.

I approach my clit cautiously because I know this thing comes on strong. When I've adjusted to the sensation enough to handle a direct assault, I press it against me, knowing this will pull me over the edge in no time, especially with his body heat radiating across me and his hooded eyes bearing witness.

My breath catches in my chest, and then it rushes out in hurried whimpers as the pleasure ratchets closer to pain, and then explodes into a combination of the two, one chasing the other again and again. The wave crests and crashes repeatedly until my clit is too sensitive to take another second of contact. I yank it away and pant through my recovery, unable to coordinate my muscles well enough to remove the thruster yet.

Dec's hand gently strokes my pussy. "Do you want me to take it out?"

"Yeah."

He pulls too softly at first, and my walls clamp to hold it in. When he tugs with more force, it slides past my resistance, releasing a pool of my arousal as it emerges. "Sweet Jesus. That is so fucking hot."

"Don't touch me there yet."

His smile is wicked. "Do you really think I can help myself? This pretty little pussy is begging to be kissed."

I'm not sure I'm ready for him, but I don't push him away when he climbs between my legs and kisses his way down my body until his tongue trails through my slit, flickering lightly over my clit. My body quivers at the touch, but relaxes when he moves his tongue lower to taste me.

Oh, fuck yes. There is nothing that could ever take the place of this.

Eating pussy has always been one of his best skills, but I'd forgotten the finer points of his master. He doesn't just thrash his tongue around; he immerses himself in it. By the time he returns to my clit, there is no sharp sting, just the sensual feel of his tongue mapping the swelling of it until every nerve ending detonates, scattering a thousand tiny deaths—something dangerous being reborn with each one. I know it even as it's happening, but I'm powerless to change it, let alone stop it.

"Fuck me, Dec."

He hoists his body up over mine and kisses me as his thick, hard cock pushes into my orgasm-cinched pussy, inching its way in, stretching me. The burn is exquisite, and the fullness feels entirely too right to be safe.

The desperate way he pumps into me, with long, hard strokes, assures me this won't be the only time he fucks me tonight. This time is for him, but he won't leave without feeling me come on his dick.

"Your cock feels so good. I love the way you fuck me."

"I love the way this perfect little snatch takes me, the way it stretches around my cock. Nothing feels better than your sweet hot cunt squeezing me. You take it all so well, baby, like you were made for me."

His hands lift my hips, and I look down to watch his dick thrusting into my pussy. "Do you like that? You like watching me fuck you?"

"Yes."

His hips jerk, and his body convulses while his deep voice gives way to feral grunts as he slams into me, and his orgasm seizes his muscles until he's spent. He lowers my hips to the mattress and collapses on top of me.

I play with his sweat-damp hair, and he shudders.

"Let's order dinner," he says. "I still owe you an explanation for some things."

"We could still go out if you want."

"Then we'd have to drive all the way home so I could fuck you again. Why would we want to do that?"

"You sure your back is going to be up for more physical activity tonight?"

"Seems like my chiropractor was right. Yoga was exceptionally good for me."

"I don't think one class could make that much of a difference."

"Then I guess you must've been the cure."

"Pretty sure your back isn't cured."

"We'll see how it feels after we eat. And how you feel about me after we talk."

"Take me to dinner. I don't know you well enough anymore to fuck you and let you get away with delivery."

Declan

SPINNING MY TEA GLASS, I wish we'd already had this conversation. I've been avoiding it, but she's nearly done eating. I'm already bargaining with myself about waiting to talk until we get back to her place, but it's only going to be harder the more time I spend with her.

"Guess I should get on with that explanation, huh?"

She pushes what remains of her salad around with her fork. I don't think she wants to talk about this any more than I do, but we both need to. "Yeah, I guess we probably have some things to say to each other."

"For starters, I'm sorry. I felt guilty when my uncle lost his contracts with your parents. He blamed me, and then I blamed myself even more. And then I wanted someone else to blame. I was a coward. By the time I pulled my head out of my ass, too much time had passed. I was sure you hated me by then."

"There was a point where I was sure I hated you, too. But your uncle shouldn't have blamed you. I'm sorry that happened."

"I knew about the policy, and I broke it, anyway. He had cause to blame me, even if he took it too far."

"It applied to me. I was their employee. I'm the one who broke it." She drops her fork. "But I never dreamed they'd fire your uncle, Dec. I expected them to fire me, not him. And I had no idea he'd fire you over it. That wasn't fair."

"I never knew I was the reason for the policy. I thought it had always been in place."

"Never let it be said my mother wouldn't go to extreme measures to get her way."

"How could she have hated me so much? She never met me."

"It wasn't about you, specifically. It was about you not ticking all the boxes on her application to date her daughter."

"You were nearly twenty-five-years-old, Carina."

"I'm well aware of how old I was. I tried so hard to have this conversation with you back then."

"I know." What else can I say to that? I already admitted I was a coward. I apologized. And now I'm getting defensive, which isn't going to help anything. My gut burns, but I take a breath and swallow a little more of my pride. "If I could go back and handle it all differently, I would."

She stares silently into the leftover lettuce on her plate.

Please say something. Don't shut me out now.

"For what it's worth, I felt guilty, too. I quit when I found out what they'd done. Walked out and vowed I'd never work for them again." I assume she's laughing at the ridiculousness of everything that happened, but then she says, "You want to hear something ironic?"

"Sure."

"A few years ago, my parents took on a partner and started acquiring larger properties. And then they bought The Nouveau, and they brought that fucked-up policy with them. The manager and maintenance supervisor were dating, but keeping it a secret as much as they could. When they got married, they went public with their relationship. What could anyone do about it at that point, right? They still got fired because my mother couldn't stand thinking she'd been outsmarted, that her authority had been dis-respected."

"But aren't your current manager and maintenance—"

"Yeah. No one bothered to tell me, but the non-fraternization policy had been canceled by the time they started working at The Nouveau. When my parents found out they were seeing each oth-er, they still tried to make it an issue, but Vaughn and Landry told them to fuck off and stay out of their personal lives. They did what I couldn't. They stood up to them."

"You did stand up to them, though. You quit. They're your parents. What you did was a lot harder." Tension creeps into my shoulders. "I never knew you did that, by the way."

"Would it have made a difference?"

"Honestly? I don't know." Damn, that's hard to admit. "I want to believe it would have mattered, but I was so overwhelmed."

"By your wounded pride."

I run my hand through my hair, search for the right words, but my well is suddenly empty. "My uncle was like a father to me growing up. I know that doesn't make the way I treated you okay, but I was gutted, Rina."

"So was I."

The hurt in her eyes is gutting me all over again. Our server drops off the check, doesn't even bother to ask if we want dessert. I don't ask either. I already know all she wants right now is away from me.

When I drop her off, I make a last-ditch effort. "I think it's shitty that your parents bought the property where you work."

"Good investment opportunity. It had nothing to do with me."

As she steps down out of my truck, I say, "Congratulations."

"For what?"

"Your promotion. You're the assistant manager now, right?"

"It's not really a big deal. Thanks for dinner."

I fully expected her to slam the door, but I still wince when she does it. I'll see her at the yoga studio on Saturday morning. If not then, I'll eventually pick the right class again.

Looks like I do yoga for the foreseeable future. Fucking namaste, I guess.

Tess would have a damn field day with this shit. My yoga schedule will remain classified information, but I'll show up for those classes.

She'll see.

Carina

THE DRIVE TO WORK goes by in a blur—the kind that makes you look up from your parking spot and wonder how you got there. Have I been replaying my dinner conversation with Declan in my head since I woke up this morning? No. No, I have not.

I've been replaying it since he dropped me off last night. I relived the whole encounter in my dreams. Stepping out of my car, I shake my head to clear away all things Declan.

We're having the pool resurfaced, and the project starts this week. Even though notices went out to every resident twice, I can count on at least half a dozen stopping by the office today to ask what's going on with the pool. At least it'll be something of the non-Declan variety to be bothered about.

The thing I hate the most is that as soon as I woke up, I immediately wondered how his back was doing and wanted to text him to ask. I had a weak moment. It could happen to anyone. But he and I burned our bridge already; there is no need to consider crossing it again.

He's sorry. I'm sorry. The whole sorry affair is over and done with. We've moved on.

But I'm not sorry about the weak moment that resulted in him being back in my bed for a few hours. Dinner was the mistake. We should've quit while we were ahead.

Landry and Molly are both already in the office. "Y'all are here early this morning." *Shit, did that sound jealous, like I think they're hanging out without me?* "I mean, not that you can't come in early without my permission."

"I wanted to be here early since it's my first day on my own," Molly says.

"Vaughn went down to meet the pool guys early, so I was awake, anyway," Landry says. "It was either work out or come in to the office."

"Really? Those were the only two choices you could come up with?" I tease. "You could've gotten us donuts."

"I have a weird feeling Autry may bring us donuts today. He hasn't been by to meet Molly yet, and that's not like him."

"You're right. Showing up with powdered donuts would be his perfect reason." I smile at Molly. "Don't feel like we're throwing you to the wolves today. You can still ask us anything."

"Thanks."

The first concerned tenant shows up before I finish my first cup of coffee. "What's going on with the pool?"

Molly looks up to handle this one. "It's being resurfaced. We sent notices out through the resident portal. If you have your notifications on, you should've received them. I'm happy to look at your account if you think there's a problem."

"Oh, I may have them turned off," the woman says sheepishly, as if she'd forgotten the resident portal even existed.

"I know it's a pain to get notifications from everywhere, but we really try to limit posts to important stuff you need to know. Or the fun stuff." Molly broadcasts her widest smile. "And we'll be using the portal to notify everyone about the pool reopening party as soon as it's ready. There will be prizes, so you might want to turn those notifications on."

"I'll definitely turn them back on. Is the pool opening going to be delayed because of this?"

"No, we fully expect it to be open by the middle of April, as usual."

"Thanks."

She turns and walks back out, satisfied with Molly's answers. I'm pretty satisfied with them, too. She handled that well. I look at Landry, and she smiles.

Molly is ready to handle simple tenant issues, which means I'm free to step into the assistant manager role fully. Landry's handled everything great, but it really is too much for one person.

So, this is it. I'm officially back in management.

Autry McDaniel swings the office door open and steps in with one hand behind his back. I don't need three guesses to figure out what he's hiding. "Good morning, ladies."

Landry introduces him to Molly. "Yes, I heard there was another beautiful face lighting up our office. These are for you. Welcome to The Nouveau." He hands her his usual brand of powdered donuts, and she fawns over them like they're her favorite thing in the world.

When he leaves, she sets the box on the back counter near the coffeemaker. "Okay, he is the sweetest little old man ever."

"He is until he has a complaint," I say. "If he's upset about something, he doesn't hesitate to let us know."

"And he can be a little harsh where Vonnie is concerned, at least in front of other people," Landry says. "But she can handle him. It's their thing."

"Got it," Molly says, blowing a puff of powdered sugar around the bite she just took. "These things are so bad they're good."

Another figure approaches the office, but I can't make out her face because it's obscured by a giant bouquet of roses. The woman peeks around the petals to be sure she's not about to run into the wall. Landry hops up and opens the door for her. "These are gorgeous!"

"Aren't they, though? Little hard to carry, but they are pretty. Are you Rina?"

"No, that would be her." Landry points to me.

I suspected they were for me the moment I saw they were peach roses, and then she announced the name on the card and removed all doubt who they're for and who they're from.

Peach roses are my favorite, and there's got to be two dozen of them in this vase. I can't see the door until I move them all the way to the opposite end of my desk.

They're beautiful. I look up to find Landry and Molly starting at me, waiting for me to read the card. "Okay, fine."

Yes, it is a big deal. Congratulations!

"He's just congratulating me on moving up to assistant manager."

"Rough hands?" Landry asks.

"You already know they're from him."

"Wow," Molly says. "That's a really expensive florist. He spent a fortune on those." She looks stunned, like she meant to think those words, not actually say them. "I'm sorry. That sounded terrible. It's just that I worked there during high school, so I know their prices. They do such good work, though."

"They do," I agree. "But speaking of work, we all have plenty, I'm sure."

"Have you seen him since he was in here?" Landry asks.

"Yes."

"When?"

"Last night."

"Where?"

"Yoga."

Molly spins around in her chair. "You go to the same yoga class?"

"It's new for him. I doubt it'll stick."

"Did you see him after yoga, too?"

Dammit, Landry. Let it go. "Yes. We went to dinner."

"When are you going to see him again?"

"I don't plan on seeing him again."

"Looks like he wants to see you again."

"You're reading way too much into it."

"Okay, sure."

I can't stop my eyes from wandering to the roses and staring at them. How much he paid for them doesn't matter to me, but they are incredibly pretty. I feel proud about being back in management now that it's official. Didn't think it would matter so much, but maybe it is a big deal. I've worked hard here.

And I really, really love these stupid flowers.

Declan

I CHECK MY PHONE for probably the tenth time this morning. She doesn't have to text to thank me for the roses, but I would like to know she got them. The florist could at least let me know.

I'm pretty sure she was lying about not loving snickerdoodles the way she used to, but I know she still loves peach roses. They're her favorites because they remind her of her grandmother—the nice one.

Rina's sentimental. No way that's changed.

My least favorite type of text from Tess comes through: the one that just says *CALL ME!*

"Rough Hands Landscaping. This is Tess."

"You rang?"

"Hey. The new guy on Rex's crew got injured. He's at the ER with him now."

"Injured how?"

"Are you sitting down?"

"I'm driving, Tess."

"Right. Okay, so apparently, he tripped over a rock while using the Weed Eater and fell. He apparently cut his arm up pretty bad on the way down."

"Bullshit! There's no fucking way that happened!"

"Hey, don't yell at the messenger. I'm just relaying what Rex told me. You might want to give him a call."

"Thanks for letting me know."

After I'm done chewing Rex's ass out for not calling me instead of the office, the truth comes out. He's already told the guy his story didn't make sense and gotten him to admit he and one of the other young guys on the crew were playing chicken with the Weed Eaters. And he was no chicken, so now he's got a goddamn spiral-sliced ham for a forearm.

"I didn't fire either one of them yet, but I assume that's what you want done?"

"Don't fire anybody until I make a phone call and confirm where we stand legally. Definitely don't fire him at the hospital!"

"Oh, yeah, that makes sense."

"Fucking kids, I swear. Were you that stupid at his age? Because I swear, I don't remember ever being that damn stupid!"

"I bet he's a little wiser right now than he was when he woke up this morning."

I can't help but laugh. "Let's hope."

"The other guy has left me two voicemails already, trying to make sure he's all right. I think they're both scared shitless, honestly."

"Good. I'll get back to you later."

As much of a dumbass as he'd have to be to not move out of the way when there's a Weed Eater coming for him, I'm already feeling bad for the kid. Both of them.

Firing young people for being careless is hard for me, even when they probably deserve it. Maybe a sliced-up arm and a good scare is enough. Fuck, I don't know. I feel like I know less and less lately.

Another text comes through. I hit the touchscreen display on my dashboard to have the bossy robot lady read it to me. She says, "Thank you for the flow-ers. They are ver-ee pret-tee."

There's no way I'm going to chance dictating my response. I pull over and type it:

> I hope your first day back in management is going well. You deserve good days and roses.

My fingers hover over my phone screen. I want to say more, but I don't want to say too much. How should I sign off? Do I just leave it? I know how I want to sign it . . . so I leave it as is and hit send.

Carina

Landry waits until Molly goes to lunch to confirm I'm still hanging out with her tonight—as if I'd cancel plans that involve wine and a new reality TV show, especially one that's been hyped the way this one has.

"Uh, hell yeah, I'm watching that with you."

"You staying over?"

"Yeah, if that's still cool."

"Of course. I just didn't know if maybe you had plans with Mr. Rough Hands."

"I do not have plans with Declan. Does Vaughn know I'm staying at your place tonight?"

"He can live without seeing me for one night."

"Are you sure?" The words are barely out of my mouth before he shows up.

Watching them flirt always makes me smile. They're so damn cute together. It almost makes me want to be in a relationship again. Not badly enough to get back on the dating apps, but almost.

Landry already has the wine opened, and she's prepping the charcuterie by the time I've changed into comfy clothes.

"I'm so excited to watch this show." She pops an olive into her mouth.

"I know." I steal a bite of cheese, and then arrange the rest on the platter she's set out. "If you hadn't introduced me to all those smutty reader groups on social media, I wouldn't be anywhere near this excited about it. But knowing we saw some of this stuff go down makes it so much better."

"I can't wait to see how they spin it."

All of our anticipation has been worth it. The first twenty minutes of the show establish it as one of the best train wrecks in the history of reality TV, and we can't stop cackling—so much so that when Vaughn walks out his door into the hallway to go for a run, he's not sure if we're having fun or being attacked.

Landry yells for him to come in because she recognizes his knock. He uses his key and steps inside. Yes, he not only has his own knock, but also a key to her place.

"Y'all should just move in together and give me this apartment," I joke.

"Ha! No way," she says. "If we ever move in together, it will be in my apartment. You can have his. I'm not leaving my bookshelves."

"Quit trying to give away my apartment," Vaughn says. "I just had to make sure y'all were okay in here."

"We're good," Landry says. "We are watching the best new show."

"It's fantastic!" I sit up straight and start filling him in. "So, this island only has one cabin on it. It's got six bedrooms. On the first day, six romance authors who bullied other authors online show up."

All they knew ahead of time was that they had to live on a remote island and write for six weeks. They each thought they were going to be the only author there, and that the whole show was going to be about them. They weren't allowed to talk about it anywhere."

Landry takes over. "Yeah, when they find out they're sharing the show with five other authors, they're pissed. Then they find out they have to work together. They have to plan a charity anthology, and each of them has to contribute a story. They're all such divas and everybody wants to be in charge and they can't agree on anything. It's great."

I top off my wine. "The best part is watching other authors and readers come together online over it. One of the authors on the island claimed she had trademarked the word eyes and had a meltdown because this new author used it in her title. Of course, everybody blew it off at first because it was obviously outrageous, but then she kept picking the newer author's book apart and editing screenshots of her replies. It got waaay out of hand. The author she bullied is commenting in real time as she watches the show, and she keeps using the word eyes in every comment!"

"And another one accused someone of plagiarism for writing a scene where a couple kisses in the rain. She insisted she invented that and no one else could use it." Landry falls back into her couch cushions, laughing as we recount the rest of the ridiculous scenarios that sound like fiction, but really happened. "Every time that author says something awful on the show or complains about how she's being treated unfairly, everybody posts gifs of people kissing in the rain!"

Vaughn shakes his head. "Someone is going to die on that island."

"No," Landy says. "I'm pretty sure the producers won't let that happen."

"But somebody might throw hands," I say. Landry and I toast to the possibility, and Vaughn lets himself out quietly, still shaking his head.

To be fair, it's not a wild guess; we've seen the previews.

The bulk of the show's marketing revolved around hints that some of the diva authors might actually turn out to be good people who made a mistake, and that at least one of them might have done everything intentionally back then, but she's changed and is a better person now. That's why most people are tuning in: to see if they agree. And to see who those fists belong to. Predictions are flying. Hands will be soon.

Everybody fucks up at some point, but some people are just fucked up. We have ten episodes to decide who's who.

Episode one ends in the expected cliffhanger. I hate that they're releasing one episode per week instead of letting us binge the whole series, but it's probably for the best. We have to work tomorrow, and we definitely would've stayed up and watched them all tonight. As it is, we can't stop talking about it.

We're finally winding down when Landry says, "You loved him, didn't you?"

"I thought I did."

"How do you feel about him now? Without thinking about everything that happened after your mom fired his uncle's company. Just your feelings about him now . . . where do they fall?"

"I don't even know him now, so I can't answer that without considering everything that happened."

"Maybe it would be worth it to get to know him again. Sure seems like he wants a second chance."

"Everybody always wants a second chance."

"That's not true. Some people just go on with their lives and never look back."

"Maybe those people are the lucky ones."

"Maybe they're assholes."

"Declan could be an asshole."

"But you won't know if you don't bother finding out."

"Goodnight, Landry."

Why can't I be one of those never-look-back people? Lucky assholes.

Landry and I are laughing in the elevator, sharing online highlights and comments from the last night's episode of *The Rest of the Story*, when I remember I have lunch plans today. "I already don't like this day."

"Why? Did the show get canceled?"

"Lunch with my mom."

"Maybe it won't be so bad. She might just want to buy you lunch and congratulate you on moving up to assistant manager."

"All your Barbies were nice to each other, weren't they?"

"You made yours fight?"

"Listen, the world's a tough place. Somebody had to prepare them."

"I'm in shock. Miss peace, love, and light made her Barbies fight?"

"That's why I'm so nice now. I got it all out of my system as a kid."

"Wait. What does that say about me since all my Barbies were friends?"

The elevator reaches the lobby and the doors open. "Draw your own conclusions, babe."

We round the corner laughing again, but I stop abruptly the moment I can see into the office.

Landry bounces on the balls of her feet. "Somebody's got an early morning visitor."

She makes me walk in ahead of her.

Before I can say a word, he says, "Go to lunch with me, Rina."

"Honestly, I'd much rather go to lunch with you than Angela, but I'm smart enough not to cancel on her."

"Tell her something came up. If she's a good friend, she'll understand."

I stare at him, waiting for him to get it.

"Oh, you meant—"

"Yeah, Angela, as in my mom."

"Well, don't tell her I'm the reason, but cancel on her, anyway."

"Stop tempting me."

"So, you're tempted? Why not follow through?"

"I haven't even had breakfast yet. I'm not prepared to execute battle strategies around lunch."

"Perfect. I'll take you to breakfast instead. I'm already here. Let's go."

Landry and I have ordered breakfast tacos to be delivered to the office. I'm looking forward to them. "I can't leave the office to go to breakfast and lunch."

"Yes, you can."

Oh, hey, have you met my manager, Friendly Barbie?

"Go. It's an order," she adds.

He doesn't need Landry egging him on. I may not know everything about Dec anymore, but I could never forget his dogged determination when he's set his mind to something. He's determined to take me to lunch—so much so that he'll settle for breakfast. We've already gone to dinner, and we both know how that ended.

I sit at my desk and drop my purse into its usual drawer. When I look up, I see six eyes staring down at me. Molly has apparently joined the side of our matchmaking manager and my ex, and they're all looming over me like they're ready to escort me out of the building. One of them literally wants to do exactly that.

The air conditioner kicks on, and the sudden current bursting from the vent over my desk ruffles my roses enough to send their scent swirling past my face. The blooms have expanded overnight. "Fine. We'll go to breakfast."

As we're walking out, Landry says to Molly, "My favorite part of playing Barbies was making Ken take her on surprise dates."

I flip her the bird over my shoulder without even looking back to see her satisfied smile.

Before the door closes, I hear Molly say, "I popped the head off every Ken doll I ever had. I just never liked his face."

Okay, now that makes me smile. I look over at Dec and realize he'd make the meanest looking Ken ever with his scruff and his perma-scowl. He has resting dick face, but I still really like it. Unfortunately, I'm still pretty fond of his dick, too.

This is going to be a long breakfast.

Declan

When I turn onto my street, she says, "Where are we going?"

Of course, she wouldn't recognize the route; I didn't live in this house when she knew me. "To breakfast."

"Is this a shortcut to a restaurant?"

"Never said anything about a restaurant. I said I wanted to take you to breakfast. Just left out the part about me cooking it."

"Because you knew I would've never agreed to it!"

I shrug. "You might have eventually agreed to it."

"Turn this truck around right now."

I pull onto my driveway, but I have no intention of backing out until after breakfast. "We're here. Let's eat."

She doesn't budge.

"This makes more sense. We don't have to wait on a table. Come on." I open my door and get out, start walking toward the house, but slowly. The sound of her getting out of my truck is all I need to hear.

Pushing the front door open, I step aside so she can walk in ahead of me.

"Nice place. Is it yours?"

"I don't own it, but my name's on the lease."

"Good to know we're not breaking into a stranger's house for breakfast."

"No way. What if they didn't have bacon?" I lead her into the kitchen and drop my keys on the counter. "Too risky."

She doesn't laugh, but I at least get a smile. It comes with an eye roll, but I'll take it.

I pull eggs out of the fridge, and she clears her throat. "Um, do I get a menu?"

"You get scrambled eggs. Unless you want them over easy or over medium. That's the extent of my breakfast cooking skills. And bacon. If the bread in my pantry isn't moldy yet, you can have toast, too."

"If the bread isn't moldy yet? I'm flattered by the amount of forethought you put into this."

"I woke up and wanted to see you. There wasn't time to go to the store." I lay strips of bacon into a pan, and then I crack eggs into a bowl.

She pours water in my coffeemaker and looks up and down the countertop. "Where is your coffee?"

"In that cabinet." I point to specify which one. "Green bag. You can't miss it."

"It stays fresher if you put it in a canister."

"I drink it every day. It doesn't have time to get stale."

"Maybe we should've gone to a coffee shop."

"Coffee shops don't have bacon."

"Um, a lot of them do, actually."

"I'm sure I'll think of something to offer you that you can't get in a coffee shop before we leave."

Another eye roll. A half-smile. She opens my fridge and pulls out a carton. "You drink toffee-vanilla creamer?"

Shit. I dated a woman for a few months who used to keep that crap here. I haven't seen her in weeks. "Check the date on that. I didn't even know it was in there."

It'll be expired for sure. At least she'll know it wasn't put in there recently.

"Still good for another few months."

Seriously? What's the damn shelf life on that stuff? Obviously longer than my relationship with the woman who bought it. "Wow. That poison must last forever."

Her indifference stings. She definitely knows another woman put that creamer in my fridge. I couldn't pretend it was mine if I wanted to.

I've never lied to her, and I don't want to start now, but whatever she's imagining is all wrong. She can pretend like it means nothing to her all she wants, but she has to be imagining something.

"No idea how long that's been in there, but it's been a while."

"You don't owe me an explanation." She shakes up the creamer and flips open the top. "Huh, it hasn't even been opened."

Before she tosses the foil seal into the trash, she runs her tongue over it to taste the creamer. My dick jumps.

"Mmmm," she says. "She has good taste."

"Had. Past tense."

"Like I said, you don't owe me an explanation."

Maybe I'm overthinking it, but that sure sounds like some aggressive coffee stirring going on behind my back as I flip the bacon.

We may not owe each other explanations about people we've spent time with over the past five years, but the coffee creamer opened the gate, and I can't lie; I'm curious about who's taken up space in her life since I gave up my place in it.

She offers to set the table.

"I've got it. Sit down. Enjoy your coffee."

I lay the bacon to drain on a paper-towel-covered plate and finish scrambling the eggs. When everything is on the table, I pour myself some coffee and sit across from her. "So, anybody leave anything personal at your place lately?"

"No, not lately."

"Anything serious over the years since we split?"

"Not really. Wasn't ever looking for anything serious." She snaps a piece of bacon in two. "How about you?"

Her answer was much shorter than I expected, and I don't know if I believe her or not. "Yeah, I had one serious relationship a few years ago."

"Coffee-creamer serious?"

"No. That one was more recent. And never serious." I take a sip of my black coffee and suddenly wonder why I felt the need to bring this up right now. This isn't what I had planned. I intended for us to have a casual, spontaneous lunch—or breakfast, as it turned out.

Seeking strength from a gulp of coffee, I swallow and then tell her the truth. "I was engaged, but it didn't work out."

"Wow. That's almost as serious as it gets."

"Almost."

"Did you live together?"

"For about a year." I hate that facial expression she just made—the one that looks like an invisible curtain has been drawn. I can still see her, but she's unreadable.

"How come it didn't work out?"

"Irreconcilable differences."

"But you tried to reconcile them?" She sets what's left of the bacon strip onto her plate. "You tried to make things work with her? You didn't just disappear one day?"

Oh, fuck. I am an idiot. "We talked it out. Realized there was no point in trying. Neither one of us was interested in changing."

"Well, at least you did that much."

"I was still learning, but yeah, I did that much."

"Do you wish you'd done more?"

"Not with her."

"I should get back to work."

"I seem to have a knack for upsetting you over meals these days. It wasn't my intention."

"I know. But I need to go. Thanks for breakfast."

"You didn't eat."

"I ate a little. I'm good."

I'm going to get this right, eventually. If she thinks I'm giving up, she's wrong.

The drive back to The Nouveau is quieter than I want it to be, but every time I think of something to say, I stop and worry it might come out wrong. The next thing I know, we're there, and I've let more time go to waste between us.

"I hope lunch with your mom goes well."

"Me, too. Thanks."

She doesn't say she'll call me to let me know how it goes, or that we should get together again soon. She just walks away. That's okay. I have her number, and she didn't say I couldn't call her.

Carina

I spend the few hours between breakfast with Declan and lunch with my mom ordering supplies online for my fledgling business. No one knows about it yet, but I've got some inventory built up—candles and bath bombs. All I need now is the guts to rent a booth somewhere to get my feet wet selling them.

It's all legitimate. I have a tax ID number and everything. My business name is Bathtub Zen. It's a play on the phrase bathtub gin, and I commissioned the cutest damn logo with a flirty little flapper in a yoga skirt, standing in one-legged mountain pose with a martini clasped in her hands, but I keep second-guessing myself.

Will people get the reference?

Is it too kitschy?

Is it just dumb?

My candles all have a different label on opposite sides of the jar. One is a standard design with my company name and logo that can be turned face-out when you have visitors who don't have a sense of humor. The other side has sayings like: *There Has Never Been a Dildo Serial Killer* and *My Pussy Doesn't Care How Big Your Truck Is.*

Both true, but lately I worry that they're not as funny as I thought they were when I came up with them.

And yet, I keep ordering supplies to make more. I use good essential oils in my scents, and I know the combinations are great, but it's a crowded market. It's not like I'd be the only one at a farmers market selling candles and bath products. But I really think mine could sell in the right place. It's not like there's only one place to buy shoes or skin care products. Lots of places sell the same type of product.

It's the brand that makes the difference, and that's what scares me. If I'm too irreverent, will people not take me seriously? I don't actually want to be taken too seriously. It's supposed to be fun.

But what if I'm straddling some weird line where I'm too crude for the Zen crowd and too woo-woo for the whiskey shooters? Honestly, that's kind of where I live, though. That's me.

I think there's room for crystals and cowgirl boots next to the same bed.

Hell, I'm not opposed to putting crystals *on* cowgirl boots. Maybe I'll sell those someday. If I ever get up the courage to sell anything at all.

My cart total is over two-hundred-dollars, and I haven't even gone to lunch with my mom yet. I probably should've saved the shopping therapy for after she's grated my nerves raw.

On second thought, I can't afford that many supplies. Besides, my apartment can only store so much.

I complete the transaction and tell myself I'm committed. This isn't a hobby. It's a business. All I have to do is open it.

It's no surprise my mother is already waiting for me at the restaurant. I'm sure she's already placed my drink order as well. There isn't a breath deep enough to steady myself for this, but I make an attempt, anyway. I start my final approach on a slow exhale.

She's been watching me since the moment I walked in, no doubt making note of my posture and my gate. I'm sure she has a few helpful suggestions at the ready. She won't drop them right off; no, she'll save them for the worst possible moment.

"Hi, mom."

"Hello, sweetheart. I love that outfit."

Wait. What? When Angela Melendez doles out compliments, it's because she wants something.

"You like what I'm wearing?" It's not exactly a power suit. I can see her appreciating black cigarette pants, but not with this white abstract floral pattern all over them. And the bright pink top I've paired them with? And for work, no less! Ha! Not buying it.

"Well, it's probably better suited for a casual activity than the office, but you wear it well. You look confident and content, and if that outfit makes you feel that way, then I'm all for it."

Oh, good. Nice to know all my existential angst is locked up tight behind my dazzling smile. Content? Sure. Who wouldn't be after the only ex they ever still think about walks back into their life, churns up their emotions like the Gulf of Mexico in a hurricane, literally rearranges their guts like only he ever could, and then apologizes for what he did as if it's the most natural thing in the world. As if we don't have enough unresolved issues to keep a therapist entertained for months.

The fucking nerve of him to just . . . apologize.

Send me roses.

Cook me breakfast.

Like he gets to decide when I should be done being mad at him.

I should've insisted on Mexican food for lunch, so we'd at least have chips on the table. I need something to crunch.

"Honey, did you hear me?" She taps her red nails on the table to get my attention.

"No, I'm sorry. It's been a busy morning. My focus is scattered." I shake my head as if my brain is an Etch A Sketch and all my thoughts will now disperse into tiny particles and settle at the bottom so I can try again. "What were you saying?"

"I ordered champagne. Just one glass each, not a bottle. But we have to celebrate your promotion."

"I've been told it's worthy of celebration."

A server sets the glasses on the table, and Mom lifts hers immediately.

I sigh internally, but I lift mine to join her toast. *Keep smiling. Just keep smiling.* My stomach is empty, and these bubbles are not going to do me any favors.

"Thanks, Mom."

"It's good to have you back in management. Landry better stay on top of her game."

"I'm not trying to take Landry's job. Assistant manager is fine with me. Leasing agent was fine with me."

"I'm not saying her job is on the chopping block, but we've always been a family-run business."

"Y'all have a partner now, Mom. An investor who is not in the family. It hasn't been a family-run business in a while. You're going to have to get used to that at some point."

"Maybe. Maybe not."

"What does that mean?"

"Our overall plans haven't changed, Carina. We just had to make some adjustments for the sake of growth. Nothing in business is permanent."

My stomach roils. I need food. Not a single thing on the menu sounds good, but no other type of food sounds good either. It's not the menu that's dulled my appetite; it's the company.

I order the chicken parmesan. It's hearty. Comfort food.

She gets a salad with grilled chicken. I know she is judging my choice. Too heavy. So much fat. But the one thing she won't offer advice on is food, because she knows I will counter with a hard sell on yoga and Pilates.

She is not a fan of exercise. It makes her nervous when I bring it up, much the same way it used to make me nervous when she'd ask me about homework I hadn't started yet or thank you cards I hadn't sent. The shame. The pressure.

There is a weird satisfaction in the full-circle aspect of it. She knows she needs to exercise, and I know she won't. Now and then, I bring it up for the sheer dopamine hit of watching her bristle and shift in her seat.

Her most strenuous physical activity is aggressively charging into meetings, flailing her arms when she bosses people around, and narrowing her eyes and clenching her jaw while she contemplates mercenary tactics.

Though if her physique is any proof, cunning greed burns some serious calories, and as long as she can still wear a size six, she thinks she's the picture of health. Never mind what her constant state of stress is doing to her on the inside. She looks good while it's happening, and that's what's important.

The chicken parm is good. Just what I needed. I finish my champagne, but I'm enjoying my food much more. So, of course, my mother has a stomach-turning declaration to make.

"I know you consider your manager a friend, but we would like you to keep an eye on the budget. She seems hell-bent on spending every dime that's allocated in every category."

"If the money's allocated in the budget, she's well within her right to spend it. She's very good at her job."

"Just because you *can* spend a little more money doesn't mean you should. I've been looking over some things and I have a few concerns, that's all. Better to pull back on the reins early before the horse completely runs away with the cart."

"You do realize The Nouveau is a luxury complex, right? Renovations don't negate the need for ongoing maintenance."

"We allowed for unforeseen expenses in the pool resurfacing, and she's nearly spent it all."

"The pool was outdated. It needed a major facelift years ago. It's customary to budget for unforeseen expenses because it's expected that there will be some. And sometimes there will be more than the estimate. You know this."

"Well, she's suddenly spending a pretty penny on landscaping as well. The grounds were entirely redone last year. How can having the grass cut and the shrubs trimmed cost so much? It's ridiculous."

"We couldn't even get a landscaping company to show up before we hired this one. And they do more than cut the grass and trim the shrubs. You know this, too."

"How did she choose this new company? Did she even get three bids? Is she related to the owner?"

"I chose the landscaping company. And I am most certainly not related to the owner."

But we have most certainly met. You've never met him, though you did fuck up his life about five years ago. You owe him this contract. Don't push me, Angela.

"You are an excellent businesswoman, mom. Micromanaging is a waste of your time. That's why you put good managers in place, and you let them do their job. You taught me that. I can't believe I need to say this, but I will not spy on Landry. I will do my job and I will do it well, just like she does hers well. The Nouveau will continue to have an excellent occupancy rate and to operate in the black. When that changes, start asking questions. Until then, continue to hone your talents in acquisitions. Worry about expanding your portfolio. Building your empire. Losing focus, taking your eyes off the prize is a dangerous thing. You taught me that, too."

"My, that was some speech."

"I have a job to get back to." I eat the last bite on my plate out of sheer spite, lift my napkin from my lap, and drop it onto the table.

I confidently stride away from the table. Some mothers would be angry if their daughters spoke to them the way I just spoke to mine. But not mine. Her pride burns so hot it's scorching my back.

She won't stop scrutinizing Landry's every decision, but she may do it more quietly now. And that should probably scare the shit out of me. My mother in crouching tiger mode can be dangerous.

We just have to be sure we give her no reason to pounce.

Declan

I DIDN'T FIRE THE kid who challenged the Weed Eater and lost, or the dumbass who stepped close enough to cut him up with it. My attorney said I could, but my conscious wouldn't let me.

Instead, I called them both into my office and let them believe I might fire them for a while, before I offered them a second chance. They just left to go join their crew for the day, and I've got no reason to stall in my office any longer.

Tess is staring at my door when I walk out. "You're such a good guy."

"Don't call me that."

Lucky for her, she has a great laugh, so she gets away with laughing in moments others wouldn't. "Keep laughing until I fire you."

She laughs harder. "So, what am I sending to our favorite client today?"

"Is it a holiday I'm not aware of?"

"No, but you've been in a terrible mood for the past few days, so I assume the roses didn't do the trick."

"I'm not trying to trick anybody into anything."

I refill my water bottle from the dispenser she ordered without my approval. She also ordered two hundred reusable water bottles with the Rough Hands logo on them and hung a sign over the water cooler that says: NO DISPOSABLE PLASTIC WATER BOTTLES ALLOWED ON THE PREMISES!

Supposedly, the reusable bottles are great *swag* for me to give customers, and the guys on our crews using them is good for business and the environment. *Win-win*, as she so enthusiastically put it.

I pick up a box of the bottles. "I guess I might as well start handing these out so we can all stop tripping over them."

"Oh, smart. Take something in person that you can give to everybody, so it doesn't look like you're there just to see her." She nods. "I mean, you're way too obvious for her not to know she's the reason, but the optics are still good."

"They don't even have this many employees. That's not the only place I'm going."

Her laughter follows me all the way to my truck.

I stop at another property on the way to The Nouveau. I'm still not sure people will give a shit about these water bottles. Call it a test run.

And I guess call it a success, because these damn bottles are a hit. Or they were there, anyway. I should've known Tess was right. She understands tangible marketing, a phrase I'd heard, but couldn't have defined until she explained it to me.

An old man in a fedora holds the front door open for me at The Nouveau. "I hope that isn't too heavy," he says.

"No. It's just full of water bottles. Thanks for the hand, though."

He looks into the box as I walk inside. "Ah, I see. Empty bottles."

"They're . . ." I cannot bring myself to utter the word *swag*. "Marketing. I own the landscaping company that's taking care of your grounds now. Just wanted to drop off a little something to say thanks to the staff."

"How nice. And I must say, your company is doing a great job. Those last fellows butchered our rose bushes. I've been sneaking them a little drink of compost tea to help them get back in shape."

"Oh. Well, thank you for taking care of them. You can stop doing that now. I promise we'll keep them fed. And we wouldn't want to overdo it."

"All right, then. I'm trusting you, young man."

"You have my word." I extend a hand. "My name's Declan. If you see me around and think there's anything I should take a look at, feel free to let me know."

He shakes my hand. "Autry McDaniel. It's a pleasure to meet you, Declan. Here, let me get the office door for you as well."

"Thank you. Would you like a water bottle?"

"Oh, that's kind of you, but I don't go in for that sort of thing."

I have no fucking idea what he meant by that, but I admire his honesty. Most people would just take it, whether they wanted it or not. Not this guy. He needs to stay the hell away from the roses, but other than, I like him.

"Can't say that I blame you. I don't really get the appeal myself, but my office manager ordered them, and people seem to like them."

"People like most anything when it's free." He opens the office door for me. "They think the whole godforsaken world is a game show, and they all want a consolation prize for getting out of bed in the morning."

"Can't argue with you about that. Thanks again."

He tips his hat and goes on his way.

Carina is staring at me. "You know Autry?"

"Just met him."

"What's in the box?"

I set it down on her desk and take out one of my consolation prizes. "I brought y'all some water bottles."

"Oh, yay!" The leasing agent flounces over to claim one. "I need a new one for the gym."

"Enjoy."

The manager comes over to take a look.

Landry, that's it. Damn, I used to be better with names. Maybe if Carina didn't work here, it'd be easier to remember the other people in the office.

"Where'd you order these?" Landry asks. "We're having a party for the residents when we reopen the pool, and these would be great for the swag bags."

Carina looks agitated, and not just at my presence. Landry's interest in these bottles clearly bothers her. "We're doing swag bags for the pool party?" she asks.

"Properties always do giveaways for resident events. We need to up our game to maintain our lease renewals. We've talked about this."

"Yeah, properties sometimes give away single items, but if they're doing bags, they usually have stuff sponsored. They don't fill them entirely from their own budget."

"Right. I didn't say we were going to do that either. But we could have The Nouveau's logo put on these and ask vendors to donate other things. I like these. They're practical."

"But probably not cheap." Carina's voice has an edge to it that sounds off, not like her at all.

She looks to me to confirm that the bottles weren't cheap, and I have a weird feeling she's also looking for me to back her up and say they're a bad idea overall. I don't know what's going on between her and her manager, but I know I don't want to be in the middle of it.

"Looks like I showed up at a good time. How about I donate the water bottles? With your logo, not mine."

Landry's face lights up. "Really? You'd do that?"

"Absolutely. I plan on working on your property for a long time to come. I'll have my office manager give you a call to coordinate it. Her name's Tess."

"Perfect. Thanks so much!"

"Happy to help."

Carina doesn't look happy about it. *What'd I do wrong now?*

I leave a few extra water bottles with them, and on an impulse before I walk out the door, I turn back and say, "Carina, you want to step outside for a bit, get some fresh air?"

"Take a break," Landry says, tipping her head sideways toward me while she stares at Carina.

I expect her to decline, but she surprises me. The moment we're out the door, she rips my head off. "What the hell was that? I know you're not doing shit like that for all your customers."

"They're not all having a pool party."

"Cute. Don't give us special treatment because of me, Dec. That was a stupid business decision. Your office manager is probably going to agree with me."

"Marketing is actually a good business decision. Necessary even."

"That's not what I meant."

"Look, you're obviously pissed off at your manager, but I have to be nice to her, regardless. She's my customer."

"I'm not pissed off at Landry."

"Are you sure?"

She sighs. "Yes. I just channeled my mother for a few minutes. God, I fucking hate when she gets in my head."

"Yeah, it didn't work out too well for me one time when she got in somebody's head, either."

"I shouldn't have brought her up. I'm sorry."

"You don't have to apologize. I'm sorry she's in a position to interfere with your job again."

"She's not. Not really. She just doesn't want to accept that, and I'm the only one she can try to manipulate. So, she tried me. And I stood up to her."

"I'm sure she didn't like that."

"Honestly, I think she loved it, which is worse."

"Buy you a drink after work? Help you get her out of your system?"

"Yeah, sure. Let's grab a drink later. Text me and let me know where to meet you."

"You can meet me at your front door at six."

"Why? I could drive myself straight from work—"

"Or I could pick you up, which is what's going to happen." I shove the box into my truck, turn around, and kiss her on the forehead. "Go be nice to your manager. I'll see you at six."

"Six-thirty."

I knock on her door at six-fifteen. If I'd let her meet me somewhere, she'd have shown up at least ten minutes late. Up to twenty minutes late is her version of being on time. She'll say I'm early, but splitting the difference between our chosen times is me being accommodating.

The door opens, and the moment I lay eyes on her, I feel all the day's stress roll off my shoulders. Her hair is down and she's still wearing makeup, but she's changed into shorts and a crop top that makes my hands twitch with the urge to hold her by the waist and pull her in for a kiss. I present the bottle of wine I brought her.

"You want to drink here instead of going out?"

"No." I laugh at myself for not realizing that's how she would interpret it. "I'm giving this to you. It's supposed to be an excellent wine, but I'm still not much of a wine drinker. It was a gift from a client. Figured you'd enjoy it a lot more than I would."

"Oh. Thanks." She takes the bottle, and I step inside and follow her to the kitchen. Her cabinets have a built-in bottle rack, but it's full.

"You need a wine cooler," I say.

"Maybe you could donate one to our resident pool party as a raffle prize. You could put the property's logo on the front of it." Her tone is pure sarcasm, but she winces as soon as she's said it. "I'm sorry. It's out of my system now, I promise."

"You always had to get that one last dig in."

"It's a character flaw. In my defense, I'm pretty sure it's genetic."

"Your positive traits always outweighed your flaws."

"Flaws? As in plural? Okay, I want to hear the list. Start."

Standing here, looking at her, I can't find a single thing to fault. Anything that may have bugged me about her before evades me completely. "Well, that overactive gag reflex was never my favorite." It really never bothered me at all, but it's all I can come up with.

Her smile is radiant. "Oh, I overcame that. There's a trick using pressure points that eradicates it completely."

Oh, now I see I mistook radiance for gloating. And I wish I could disguise my jealousy at the possibility she might be serious. If she learned to overcome it, she did it with someone else, and I irrationally want to pummel a potential stranger right now. "Well, good for you."

"Eh, I don't know how good it's been for me, but it seems to have been great for others."

"Are you done?"

"Are you mad?"

"Getting there."

"Then yes, I'm done."

She turns to head for the door, but I grab her by the waist to stop her. I lift the back of her hair and kiss her neck. "Show me."

"Before you've even bought me a drink?"

"Demonstrate using your fingers."

"My fingers are actually required." Her left hand goes up, and her thumb bends in to meet her palm, her fingers folding over it tightly. She counts off five seconds. With her left hand still clenched in a wrongly made fist, she presses the tip of her right index finger firmly against her chin. Again, she slowly counts to five. There's no way this works. I think she's making it up as she goes to fuck with me, but I'm amused enough to keep watching over her shoulder. Then she opens her hand and uses her right index finger and thumb to pinch the fleshy web between her left index finger and thumb for five seconds. When she releases that, she exhales, turns to face me, and immediately sticks two fingers so far down her throat my dick surges against my zipper.

She pulls her fingers out of her mouth and smiles. "See? No gag reflex. What are you in the mood for? I'm thinking martinis sound good."

I've missed everything about her, but this playful, flirty side most of all. She could always get to me when she teased. Sometimes, she'd push my buttons in ways that would piss me off if anyone else did it. She knew she could get away with it, probably even make me smile and forget what I was mad about in the first place.

But when she teased like this, when it was undeniably sexual . . . she owned me, just like she does right now.

I'll drink whatever the fuck she wants.

Carina

MOST PEOPLE WOULD SAY that Dec has a nice smile, but when it's got that mischievous quirk to it, and his eyes take on that wicked glimmer, there is nothing nice about it. That's blatant notice of his intention to be bad.

And an open invitation to join him.

I tell myself what I'm feeling as I sit across from him in this leather booth, sipping my extra dry martini, is nothing more than memories. He's conventionally attractive in the most hetero-normative way possible. That's all I feel for him anymore: basic sexual attraction. Barely even that.

My libido laughs in wet panties.

Fine. Strongly. I feel it strongly! He's hot. I'm human.

He insisted we come to a steakhouse for happy hour. Which they don't have, by the way. I tried to tell the server we're only having drinks, but he brought us dinner menus, anyway. And I am hungry.

We've attempted this eating together thing twice already, and it hasn't turned out great yet. Maybe this will be one of those third-time's-the-charm situations.

The bartender got my martini order perfectly right: extra dry, extra olives, brine on the side. Our server didn't even flinch at the special requests. If I'd known Dec was going to insist on coming here, I'd have changed clothes. And he would've said, "My money spends the same no matter what we're wearing."

He's that guy. Wants to live entirely by his own rules. He'd come in here in sweatpants and not feel an ounce of self-consciousness. Tonight, however, he's in dark jeans, a white button-down, and boots.

The candle on the table has nearly burned out. I'll be able to relax more once the flame is fully extinguished. It's a silly little thing, but it's just too romantic. We are not candlelight and roses, not anymore. Okay, he sent me roses. The most beautiful roses I've ever seen. But the only candles I care about right now are the ones I'm pouring and trying to convince myself to sell.

If I told him about Bathtub Zen, he'd probably encourage me to go for it. I know he would. Part of me wants to blurt out every detail, how hard I've worked on the branding and product creation and all my plans for future products.

But that's my biggest secret, my most personal thing, and I'm not ready to let anybody else in on it. Even Landry doesn't know. And she's never broken my heart.

Our steaks arrive, and mine is perfectly done, just like my first martini. I've ordered a second. I may order dessert, too.

"What are you thinking so intently about?" he asks.

"Me? Nothing really." I finish my martini. *Bring on that second one, please.*

"I can see the gears turning behind your eyes, Rina. You've got something on your mind. Wanna share?"

"No." I say it as nicely as possible, but it's still a harsh response.

"Okay. Fair enough." He spoons roasted potatoes onto my plate. "You've gotta try these."

This is the kind of place where the food tastes so good you can't help but wonder if it's because of where you're eating it. Like, am I impressed because of the chandelier that's sparkling in my peripheral vision or because they've really worked some magic on these simple potatoes? Would I like them this much anywhere else? With anyone else? Because maybe that matters, too.

"They're good," I agree. "How's your steak?"

"Great. Yours?"

"Great."

Oh, no. This suddenly has such an awkward first-date vibe. It wasn't supposed to be a *date* at all. Just drinks. Sharing about our week. Like friends. Or people who could potentially become friends once we leave all our past bullshit in the past.

We could get there. Over drinks, not dinner with a candle on the table and a thousand tiny glimmers overhead, winking like cheeky little fucking stars. Like I could make a wish . . .

"You still doing fishing tournaments?" My new martini arrives, and I carefully pour in the brine and give it a gentle stir with my skewer of olives.

"Not as often as I used to. The business took off. Life got busy."

"So, if I looked at your profile on a dating app, you're telling me I wouldn't see a picture of you holding a fish?"

"You won't find me on a dating app to begin with."

"Were you ever on them?"

"Yeah, for a while. I tried it. Didn't like it."

"If I found an old profile, would there be a picture of you holding a fish?"

He laughs. "You just have to make me say it, don't you? I don't remember, but there is a possibility I may have been that guy. But in my defense, those were really the only pictures I had. What was I supposed to do, take a selfie in the bathroom mirror? Or at the gym? Are those any better?"

"No." I laugh with him. "They're really not any better."

"What does your profile picture look like in the online meat market?"

"That is such a gross description." I try my fresh martini. "Accurate, but gross. And I'm not on any dating apps anymore either."

"But when you were?"

"I don't know. Just a headshot."

"Really? No sideways full-body shot with your leg bent and your head tilted?"

I laugh hard at that. "Wow. Somebody took notes."

"It seems like every woman has taken some notes on that pose. Do they teach y'all that in college or something?"

"Are you kidding? High school. If you haven't mastered it by college, you'll probably die alone. Or at least be responsible for all your own orgasms."

"I think I was responsible for all my own orgasms in college."

"Um, yeah, I know for a fact you were not."

His eyes widen. "Shit, that's right. I was still working on my degree when we were dating."

"I'm pretty sure you weren't suffering through solo orgasms before you met me, either."

He shrugs. "I mean, some of them."

"Did you meet your fiancée online?"

"No. Mutual friends introduced us."

"Are you still friends?"

"Yeah. It's not their fault it didn't work out." His eyes meet mine as the candle on the table flickers out. "Oh. You meant me and her, didn't you?"

"Yeah."

"I wouldn't say friends, but we're friendly if we run into each other. It happens. We still have some of those mutual friends, so she and her husband show up places."

"She's already married to someone else?"

"They seem great together, to be honest. I'm happy for her."

"Never jealous at all?"

"You are probably the only woman I ever really felt jealous of. Despite all your insistence that it was toxic and damaging to carry it around. It's still there a little. I don't like thinking about you with other men since we've been apart." He holds up his hands in defense. "I know. I know. I'm the one who walked away. It's none of my business what you've done since. Or who you've done it with. But I don't have enough peace in my aura or whatever to *let that shit go*." His hands are still up, and he puts air quotes around the end phrase.

Hearing words like *peace in my aura* come out of his mouth will never not be funny to me. Let alone hearing him say *let that shit go*. He has never been a *let that shit go* kind of guy.

That's why it was so hard when he let me go. On the bright side, I just got a new candle label out of it. I'm definitely making one that says I Don't Have Enough Peace in My Aura to Let That Shit Go. It'll probably be my biggest seller.

"Haven't seen you at yoga again. Did you switch studios?"

"It didn't really do anything for me."

"Excuse me? I distinctly remember a claim about it curing your back. It did something for you, Dec. It helped."

"I don't like not knowing what I'm doing, okay? I felt ridiculous. We started out facing one way, and the next thing I know, we'd turned around and I was on the wrong foot with the wrong arm out like a dumbass."

"If it didn't come easy, surely it's not worth trying again."

He stares at me. "We are still talking about yoga, right?"

"Are we?"

"If we're not, then I need you to know that I wholeheartedly believe it's worth trying again."

"We can't just jump back into a relationship."

"I never meant to imply we could. But could we try? Start slow and get to know each other again?"

One and a half perfectly mixed martinis is apparently the magic number of martinis to melt the lock on the titanium box around my heart. My eyes are threatening to leak at the prospect of saying yes to his request. "We'd have to take it slowly."

"You can set the pace. I'll follow your lead. If I move too fast, you say the word and I'll back off."

"No, you won't."

"I'll try. My intentions will be good." He asks for the check.

The ride back to my apartment is as quiet and tense as when he drove me back to the office after breakfast.

Did I really agree to . . . what, exactly? Dating him? We never actually said dating. He said get to know each other again. So, we're going to be friends first? Maybe friends only, depending on how it goes. Maybe less.

I reach for the door handle when he parks, and he laughs. "I'll come around and open your door for you. You don't have to leap out, do you?"

"We're just getting to know each other again."

"When we were first getting to know each other, didn't I open your car door? Didn't I walk you to your front door? I can still do those things now, right?"

"I can open this door and get out of the truck on my own. But you can walk with me."

"Okay."

Cicadas serenade the courtyard as we walk toward the stairs that lead to my front door. It's March in Houston, so the temps are bouncing from warm to cold and back again. It was a warm day, but there's a slight chill in the air tonight, enough to spread goosebumps over my arms and legs. The scent of Dec's cologne is in the wind, too.

He takes my hand, and I let him because his is warm. And because I want him to touch me. The closer we get to the stairs, the more I want to invite him in. That only ends one way—and we still know each other quite well in that way. No need to get reacquainted on that front.

At the top of the stairs, he squeezes my hand. At my door, he says, "How long does that pressure point trick last on your gag reflex?"

"Not long. I'd have to do it all over again." I turn my key in the lock. "It's a lot to ask a girl you hardly know."

"What if I promise to let that shit go? Can I come in?"

"Can I trust you to be a gentleman?"

He puts his hands against my door to box me in with his arms, his chest pressing against my back, letting his breath steam my ear as he whispers, "Not even a little bit."

I tilt my head to smile up at him, and he kisses me as I push the door open.

We stumble into my bedroom, half-entangled in a frenzy of kissing and unbuttoning each other. We disengage long enough to kick off our shoes and rip off our clothes. I walk backward toward the bed, but he grabs me and spins me before I reach it. "No. I want you on top. Show me what yoga can do. Sell me on the benefits."

"You've seen my ass."

"I said sell me on *yoga*." He pulls me down on top of him.

"Yoga built this ass."

"Sold. See you in class." His hands glide down my sides, following the dip of my waist and reaching around to squeeze my butt cheeks. "I love yoga."

I sit up and straddle him, locking my thighs and hovering my pussy over him without moving into position to take him, staying just close enough for him to feel the heat, to imagine the moment of entry, and then I hold up my left hand. My thumb stretches across my palm and then disappears behind my folded fingers.

"One deep-throat blow job. Two deep-throat blow jobs. Three deep-throat blow jobs. Four deep-throat blow jobs. Five deep-throat blow jobs." Mississippi didn't seem like the right word for this countdown. I still used four syllables. Bound to be the equivalent of a second, right?

His wicked smile is back. I sink down a few inches and wiggle a little, brushing my vulva ever so slightly across his engorged dick as I bring the tip of my right index finger to my chin and repeat the count. His cock twitches when I open my left hand and spread my fingers.

I enunciate every syllable on the final count while I pinch my hand. When I exhale, I make sure it's so very exaggerated.

And then I reach for his cock and press the tip inside my pussy.

"Wh-wha-what?" His breath comes out like someone is performing chest compressions on him.

I match his wicked smile. "Is this not what you wanted?"

"I'm never not going to want what you're about to do, but you are an evil, evil woman."

"Aw, why would you judge me so harshly?" I slide down onto his cock on a prolonged gasp. His body jolts under me, and he moans. No more complaints. Planting my feet on either side of him, I show him exactly how good yoga has been for my quads.

His eyes smolder as he watches my pussy stretch to take him, sliding up and down, coating him with my juices. A shiver wracks his shoulders and runs down his back. That's my cue to dismount.

"No, no, no, no." He reaches for me, but I move out of reach.

And then I climb between his legs on my hands and knees. "I thought you wanted to see how well the pressure point thing worked. No? Did I get that wrong?" I run my tongue up the length of his erection.

He shoves his fingers into my hair and pushes my face downward when I reach the tip.

It's difficult to make good on the promise of a gag-free blow job while laughing, but I give it my all—tears leaking from my eyes, saliva spilling from my mouth, moaning to create a gentle vibration. It's enough. He doesn't last long enough for my gag reflex to reactivate.

Mission accomplished, even with a teasing pre-show attraction.

I swallow all he's got to give and smile up at him. "I got that from yoga, too."

"Seriously?"

"Yeah, there's a special class for it. We practice on the person next to us."

"Okay, smartass."

"I don't know if I should be impressed with my own acting skills or worried about your lack of critical thinking skills right now."

"I wasn't exactly in an analytical headspace when you said that."

"What kind of headspace are you in right now?"

He pulls me up and flips me onto my back. "Ladyhead? Is that the right space?"

"Sounds like the right answer to me."

Declan

THE SIGHT OF HER lying here with her legs spread brings back more than memories. There's an overwhelming rush of familiarity that isn't just about what was, but what almost was, what could've been.

We were on the brink of being so much more when it all went wrong, but right now, that feeling of everything being so damn right again is strong enough to stitch us together as if the past five years never happened.

Our time spent apart doesn't matter when we're together like this.

My tongue touches her delicate skin, and she trembles. That first taste of her ignites a need for more, just like it always did. I settle in and lick through her seam, trailing back down and flattening my tongue, teasing around her opening before letting my tongue slide inside.

Her hips tilt to welcome my mouth. When I move up to trace around her clit, she pulls her hips back slightly. She's not trying to escape; it was an instinctive reaction, a response to her nerves being stimulated.

I drape her legs over my shoulders so she can't move away and seal my mouth against her as I begin to lick and suck on her clit. God, I love when she starts to squirm while her clit swells under my tongue.

I'm instantly hard again, but I won't fuck her until she comes. When I draw her clit into my mouth this time, I don't let up to tease her with licks and caresses anymore.

Her thighs pull together, pinning my face between her legs, but I keep her pussy open and exposed to me using nothing more than my mouth. I slide my hand into place to slip two fingers inside her tight, silky cunt.

The quivering starts in her glutes and spreads to her legs. Shallow breaths punctuated with sharp, high-pitched yelps let me know she's there, and then her juices flow around my fingers, creamy and releasing a softly sweet, tangy scent that makes my mouth water and my dick twitch.

I release her clit and dip down to taste her pussy once more before I rise and press my fingers to her lips. She opens her mouth and sucks her arousal off my fingers, turning my cock to granite.

There are always times, after you've been together for a while, when you take fucking each other for granted, but I can't imagine now how I ever could have with her. The way her pussy is stretching around my cock as I push inside her feels closer to sacred than anything else I've ever known.

The words on the tip of my tongue would ruin everything, but I can't think of a better time to say them, so I kiss her instead. And I don't take a moment of it for granted.

I'm unsettled when my eyes open. Her dark hair fanned across her pillowcase reminds me where I am. The shock of having spent the night here makes me wonder if I should sneak out. Who fell asleep first? Did she mean to let me stay?

She peeks at me through her eyelashes without fully opening her eyes. "What time is it?"

"I think my phone is in my pocket, which is on the floor . . . somewhere." I blink sleep from my eyes and look around the room.

Her drowsy laugh is sexy. She slips out of bed and walks to my jeans. My eyes outline her curves as she bends over to pull my phone from my pocket. "Here. I'll go make coffee." I catch my phone, but it requires some extended effort. Her toss is off the mark by several feet, but the required lunge is worth it to hear her laugh again.

My eyes are glued to her firm, full ass as she walks away, and my dick says we need that more than we need coffee, but I know better than to push my luck. The fact she's offering me coffee instead of kicking me out feels like a gift.

I get up and put my clothes on. Sitting on the edge of her bed, I spot an entire shelf of the same candle. My first thought is that it must've been a good sale, maybe her favorite scent or something . . . but then my eyes distinctly make out the word pussy on one of the labels.

Color me curious.

The full text of the label is My Pussy Doesn't Care How Big Your Truck Is. I pick one up and realize there is a label on the opposite side of the jar as well. It's a logo for a company called Bathtub Zen. *Huh.*

She's rummaging through her fridge still naked when I enter the kitchen. Fucking perfection. "So, what does it take to impress your pussy?"

There is a stick of butter in her hand when she spins around. "What?" Her eyes lock onto the candle in my hand. "Oh."

"Why do you have so many of these?"

Her lips are tight and her shoulders tense. She doesn't want to tell me, and I should respect that and leave it alone, but I want to know, so I ask again.

"Because they're mine."

"Okay. But why'd you buy so many? Was Bathtub Zen going out of business or something?"

"No." She slaps the butter onto the counter. "You have to be open for business before you can go out of business."

It takes a few seconds for me to understand. "Is it your business?"

She shrugs and her gaze drops to the floor. "It will be. I just have to work out a few more details."

"You make candles. Is this the only one?"

"How could I open a business with only one product?"

"Can I see the rest?"

"It's not just candles. I make bath products, too."

"Ah, the name makes more sense now." I smile at her, but she looks like she'd rather fall through a trapdoor than talk about this. "Are you opening a store?"

"I'll probably just start out selling at farmers markets. Maybe an online shop at some point."

"That's cool. You were always artsy."

"Yeah, I guess so."

"You put butter in your coffee these days?"

"I was going to offer you breakfast, but I don't have any eggs. Or bacon. Want some toast? My bread's not moldy, I promise."

"I'd love some toast."

"Okay. I guess I should get dressed first."

"Why ruin breakfast with clothes?"

She smirks as she walks past me, and then she backtracks and takes the candle from my hand. "Coffee's ready. Help yourself."

I pour myself a cup, and then I wander down the hall to find her already wearing a sweatshirt and leggings, putting all the candles in her closet. "Hey, I'm sorry. I didn't mean to intrude on something you didn't want to share."

"It's okay. I shouldn't have just had them out on display."

"Why not? It's your personal space. But I wish you didn't feel like you had to hide something like that. You should be proud."

"Of what? Some stupid candles I might never sell."

"What's stopping you?"

"I don't know, okay? It's just . . . what if there's not even a market for them?"

"Did you do any research?"

"Yes. I'm not a complete idiot. This type of thing sells in a lot of places, but there's no guarantee mine will sell."

"Very few things in life come with a guarantee, but that doesn't mean you shouldn't try."

Our eyes meet, and I know she thinks I'm talking about us, but I'm genuinely talking about her believing in herself. "If you rent a space or set up a website and try to sell your products, I'll try yoga again."

"Will you keep doing yoga for as long as I keep trying?"

"Yes. You don't give up on . . ." I pause to read the label again. "Bathtub Zen, and I won't give up on yoga."

"I feel like you just tricked me into this, but I know how badly you need yoga, so it's a deal."

"Good. But tell the truth, you really like my big truck, don't you?"

"I'm not taking my clothes back off."

"You can't blame me for trying. What do your other candles say?"

She steps inside her closet and emerges with a different jar. I turn it until I can read the alternate label. "Are there people saying women will die if they use dildos?"

"You were thiiiiiiis close." She holds her thumb and index finger a few inches apart. "The intended commentary is that dildos are safer than men."

"Ohhhh. In my defenses, I'm probably not your target audience."

"Probably not."

"Are your bath products anti-men, too?"

"My products are not anti-men. They're pro-women."

"Me, too." I pull her in for a kiss.

Carina

MOLLY LOOKS UP FROM her desk when I swing the office door open and step inside. There's a chill in the air, and it's not from the air-conditioner.

Her usual smile is missing, which makes me realize how stupid-huge mine is. It's not that I don't normally smile in the mornings, but I'm floating into work today like Reese Witherspoon just praised my bath salts on TikTok.

All it really took was Dec encouraging me to go for it with Bathtub Zen. I'm ready now. If it doesn't take off, oh, well. At least I'll be able to say I tried.

But Molly looks like she's ready to punch a wall.

"You okay?"

"I hate the woman in 501."

"She needs a lot of attention. What happened?"

"She put in a maintenance request, saying her tub wasn't draining—"

"Yep, that's one of her staples."

"Holden went up to take care of it for her. He says she seemed fine while he was there, but then she called the office and went off on me for five minutes about sending an *underling*, whatever the hell that means, to handle an ongoing issue. He's maintenance. Who was I supposed to send?"

"Vaughn."

"Only Vaughn can respond to her requests?"

"As much as he hates the fact, yes. It makes all our lives easier. She has a thing for Vaughn. He doesn't love responding to her, but he can handle her. And every new chance to impress him thrills her."

"Does she know about him and Landry?"

"She prefers to ignore that. I think she really believes she'll win him over one day."

"Holden and I were the only ones here, and I thought I was helping by taking care of it."

"We should've warned you. Don't take it personally. Sometimes, Vaughn's busy and he sends Holden to her apartment. It wasn't the first time she'd met him. She's harmless, just smitten with Vaughn. Some people like a challenge."

"I hope she's harmless."

"Like I said, she needs attention." I fill Molly in on some of 501's previous antics, like the time she took her top off at the pool, and another tenant called the cops on her for public indecency.

"Great. Can't wait for the pool to reopen."

"Anything else going on?"

"Oh, yeah. I almost forgot. Vonnie left a message to say she likes rosé now. She says it's very trendy, so you might want to get some for the office."

I laugh and try not to end up gargling my coffee. "Vonnie's helpful like that. I wonder where she had rosé. Guess I'll pick up a box. My mother should love that."

"Why? Is your mom a big fan of boxed rosé?"

Molly doesn't know my parents are part owners of The Nouveau. I honestly wish no one knew. "She's a businesswoman who hates frivolous expenses."

Completely accurate statement.

Landry shows up and saves me from any further conversation about my mom. She stops halfway to her desk and stares at me.

"What? Why are you looking at me like that?"

"You look suspiciously happy this morning."

"She came in looking that way," Molly says.

"Why is it suspicious for me to be happy? I'm always happy."

"Sure. Anything urgent going on this morning?"

"501 is mad because Molly sent Holden to unclog her drain. And Vonnie would like us to stock rosé in the fridge from now on."

"I wonder where she had rosé."

"That's what I said. But I added it to my list."

"Does she like bubbly or non-sparkling?"

I turn to Molly, who shrugs.

"Better get both," Landry says.

My jaw clenches a little. I wish it didn't, but getting both seems ridiculous. Why not just buy bottles of champagne by the case? We already keep a box of red and a box of white. There isn't room for four boxes of wine in the fridge.

Okay, technically, we have plenty of room, but all I can think about is my mom showing up and looking in there to find that many boxes of wine. Four? Angela would blow a fuse. At Landry. And at me for letting it happen. Dammit! I'm not the company snitch.

And a few more boxes of wine won't bankrupt The Nouveau by any means. I take a deep breath and tell myself to let that shit go.

New candle label? *Buy another box of wine and let that shit go.* Hmm, I like it.

Is it too much to have two labels with "let that shit go" mentioned? I think there's definitely room for two. Maybe three. Should there really be a limit on letting shit go?

It's highly possible that limitations should top the list of shit I need to let go. But where is the limit on letting go of limits? Well, this will be on a fucking loop in my head for the rest of the day.

A delivery person walks in with a wide grin on his face. It's apparently a good day for smiling. "Which one of you beautiful ladies is Rina?" He giggles like he's being tickled by invisible hands. Yeah, okay, there's a good chance he's smiling because he's high. Too high.

Landry and Molly point at me. Being stoned is not at all the reason for their grins.

"That would be me."

He steps forward and drops a bag onto my desk. "Hope you like chocolate." Again with the giggles. "Enjoy." He chuckles all the way out the door.

The word chocolatier dances across the dark blue bag in shiny gold font with swirls and flourishes. There is a card sticking out of the top. I have a feeling I'd rather wait to read it at home, but Molly and Landry are giddily waiting for me to confirm who sent the candy.

Speaking of people who need more limitations. I open the card and tell them what they already know. "It's from Declan."

"What's the occasion?" Molly asks.

"I think the occasion is her." Landry laughs.

She's wrong though. He had a more specific reason. The card says:

I bet the owner of this place questioned if a chocolate shop was a good idea before he opened it. Maybe he almost didn't. But he did. I stood in line for thirty minutes to buy this candy. Sometimes unlikely things work out.

He's no more subtle than Vonnie. And his double meaning is clear. Yeah, longshot business ventures sometimes turn out to be successful, but he's talking about our relationship, too.

I know there's a chance that things could work out between us, but we have a history that's not all not sunshine and smiles. That's not going to magically fade away.

Taking it slow and getting to know each other again is the only way we have a chance. So far, it's hard not to like the current version of Dec. But he has his flaws like anyone else. It's easy to stick around and shower someone with gifts and good times when things are new. Or new again.

I spread chocolate bars and truffles across my desk. Landry pulls on the ruffled ends of a truffle wrapper to spin it open.

As if she could sense me thinking about her (she can, I swear), Vonnie shows up with Lolita securely wrapped around her. The snake's tongue flickers up and down, grabbing chocolate molecules from the air.

"Ah, sweets from your ex, I assume?"

Landry raises an eyebrow. "Are we still calling him your ex?"

Vonnie considers the variety of chocolate on offer. "Whatever we're calling him, he spent a few dimes on this haul. Want to hear my guesstimate?"

"No, thank you," I say. "We're getting to know each other again. That's all."

Peering inside to gauge the amount of chocolate still left in the bag, Vonnie says, "Girl, you must have no gag reflex at all."

Molly spits water onto her desk.

"She knows a pressure-point trick to deactivate it," Landry says.

"It's mind over matter," Vonnie says, now lifting the bag to check the weight. "Always has been, but if it takes some ritual to clear your mind so you can handle the matter, hey, whatever works."

"Would you like some chocolate, Vonnie?"

"I'll take this hazelnut espresso bar off your hands." She waves it in the air. "Did you get my message about the wine?"

"I did. I've added your request to my shopping list. Do you prefer sparkling or non?"

"Oh, I didn't know it came in a sparkling version. Hmm, I do enjoy a little bubbly on occasion. You better get one of each."

Landry nods. "That's what I said."

"Clearly, I'm raising you right." Vonnie taps her on the shoulder with the candy bar.

They all laugh. I cringe internally, knowing the woman who raised me etched far more practical lessons into my psyche. But I think there's a fine line between exercising caution and being paralyzed by it. I wish it were brighter, flashing in neon, anything to make it more obvious.

The older I get, the less clear it is whether my mother operates on the advantage of wisdom and experience or cowers on the knife-edge of fear, afraid to take a risk too big. She always said my free-spiritedness must've been caused by a weak link in our DNA. It's a cruel comment, but she never saw it that way. Failure is her biggest fear. Being afraid of it is mine. We are not the same.

So why am I scrutinizing the cost of boxed wine on her behalf?

I unwrap a triple-dark truffle. It's rich and smooth, not too sweet, but not bitter either. Perfectly balanced. Totally worth however many dimes it cost. But I still don't want to know the number.

The owner of the pool company walks in, shaking his head. I eat another truffle as he explains to Landry that we have an electrical problem. They can't proceed with the new lights without an electrician. She asks how much he thinks it will cost to fix it.

His estimate leaves me reaching for a third piece of chocolate.

"This is going to delay the project, isn't it?"

"Probably by a few weeks."

Out in the lobby, I see Vonnie talking to her supposed nemesis, Autry McDaniel. I watch her open her chocolate bar and break off a piece. She hands it to him with a smile. He takes a bite and returns her smile, stepping closer to her as the chocolate melts on his tongue.

For a moment, I think they might kiss. Lolita extends her head and darts her forked tongue between them. Autry jerks back and glowers.

Vonnie pulls the snake's head close to her cheek. I don't have to hear her words to know they're not friendly. A disparity in serpent love has quashed the magic spell of expensive chocolate.

They'll reconcile, probably when no one is looking, but for now, Autry walks away without even tipping his fedora. Vonnie turns toward the elevator, and the smile on her face could be seen from the moon.

Vonita Viper may have left the stage, but she's still a performer. She deserves two kinds of pink wine.

Declan

I PULL INTO THE parking lot of the yoga studio and scan for her car before I park. It's not here, but I'm early. I need to borrow one of the studio's mats again. I'm not buying my own. This is temporary. As soon as my back is better, I'm done with downward dogs and warrior whatevers.

The girl at the front desk recognizes me. She's apparently good with names. "Hi, there. Welcome back, Declan!"

"Thanks."

There must be a class still going on because the door to the practice room is closed.

"You can go on in. Just be sure to close the door behind you. We don't want to let the heat out." My face must convey my confusion because she goes on. "This is going to be a hot class. You knew that, right?"

"How hot?"

"It won't exceed a hundred and five."

"Degrees?"

She giggles. It's cute, but my question was serious.

"Yes, but don't worry. We have humidifiers going so it's not too dry. If this is your first hot class, grab a spot by the door, just in case you need to step out, but you probably won't. Jen knows what she's doing, and she'll watch out for you. Make sure you have water."

I glance at the front door.

"Don't leave," she says. "You're going to love it!"

That's an overstatement. I might survive it, but there's no way I'm going to love it.

Not sure how I missed that this was a hot class, but I bet I won't miss that detail in the future. Fuck it. I'm already here. Why not?

I slide the door open enough to step into the room. Or more accurately, the oven. Who came up with this? It feels like a scam. I roll out a mat near the door and look around at the other early birds. They're all sipping water and stretching. Seems like a good idea. I drink some water, debating whether I'm really going to stay.

The guy in front of me folds forward and his chest literally lays flat against his knees. That's not normal. I don't think the human body is supposed to do that.

When I hinge forward at the waist, I can barely lower a third of the way, and I feel every inch of the stretch in my lower back and my hamstrings.

Soft fingertips tap my shoulder. "Hi," she says. "I'm Jen. Elle says this is your first hot class."

"Yeah. I didn't realize what I was getting into."

"You'll catch on easily. Listen to your body. If you feel light-headed or nauseated, sit on your mat and sip some water. Try not to leave the room unless you absolutely have to. Your body will adjust to the heat. It's super good for your muscles and your organs. I'll be explaining the benefits as we move through the poses. Welcome to your first hot yoga class, Declan."

These people are big on names. I've already forgotten hers. "Do you know if Carina comes to this class?"

"Oh, you know Carina? I love her. She used to come to my hot classes, but I think she's switched her practice to mostly flow and Ashtanga."

Perfect. I'll be switching mine to those, too.

With a gentle pat on my shoulder, she says, "You're going to be addicted to Bikram before you know it."

I don't even know what that means, but I'm not really looking to pick up an addiction right now, thanks.

A sideways look at the humidifier next to me tells me the room is at forty percent. The class hasn't even started yet and I'm sweating, but it is getting easier to breathe the heavy air. I'm choking on anxiety, though. I hate this shit already.

Why didn't I pay better attention to the schedule? How many damn kinds of yoga are there?

Maybe it's for the best that Carina's not here to witness this.

This breathing exercise is weird.

Twist my arms which way and my legs how? I watch Captain Elastic in front of me and copy his position. I can't morph into a damn human pretzel like he can, but I'm in the right general contortion. My balance sucks, but I'll strain every muscle in my body before I'll fall down in front of all these people.

Is there not a single pose where both feet can stay on the ground?

Okay, good. I can't squat that low, but at least I can plant my feet to balance for this one.

I wonder if there's a type of yoga where you face the same direction the whole time, because this turning around bullshit feels like a trap to see if you're paying attention.

The instructor says we're done with the standing exercises and moving to our mats for the second half of the class. She can't mean we're only at the halfway point. Surely, she used that as a figure of speech.

There's so much sweat dripping off my body, I look like I just climbed out of a pool. Why is there no clock in here?

Some of these poses are more likely to break my back than heal it. This is a one-and-done class for me.

Okay, I recognize that word she just said. It means it's over. Now we just lie here for a little while.

Supposedly, this is when the healing happens. It's when my gratitude happens, I know that much.

My breathing calms. I'm still sweating, but I feel okay. Almost good even. I never ended up facing the wrong way in this class. And I didn't die, so there's that.

We file out of the room. And there she is, storing her shoes and purse for the next class. Of course!

She looks up and catches me staring at her. "You're doing hot yoga now?"

"Not intentionally."

Her laugh is contagious. "You're going to sleep so good tonight."

"You mean pass out?"

"You'll be fine. The hard part's over. Drink lots of water."

She walks past me to the water dispenser. I stall for a minute to see if she'll come back over, but another woman strikes up a conversation with her, and they walk off together.

It's been a long time since I've literally had to peel sweaty clothes off my body. Every inch of fabric is still soaked. A hot shower zaps the last of my energy.

My muscles are loose, but my body is exhausted. I eat cold leftover pizza at my kitchen counter, wishing I'd chosen the class Carina took tonight. That heat may have done me some good, but I'd have rather been watching her body shift into poses. She makes it look effortless.

Everything always felt easier when I was with her. The stress of balancing school and work faded. I believed I could achieve all my goals because she believed. It was all so much harder after I shut her out.

But tonight, on the way home from yoga, an asshole cut me off in traffic and I didn't flip him off, didn't cuss him out through the windshield. No anger at all.

She'd credit yoga, but I know it's all her.

Carina

I'VE TRANSFORMED MY BEDROOM floor into an assembly station. I poured candles all day today, and they're finally cool enough to label. Rows of jarred candles line the rug. I have a system: put a label on four, stack them in a box, move down a few feet to label the next four, and repeat the process until I have them all labeled and boxed.

It's tedious work, but it has to be done. Having boxes of candles instead of a single shelf makes Bathtub Zen feel like an actual business, even though I haven't sold a single one yet.

Tomorrow, I'll be making bath bombs and sending emails. I've chosen my first-choice farmers market. There are a few local shops that take products like mine on consignment. I made a list.

Once I started boxing and stacking, there was no going back. There's a maze of boxes between my closet and my bathroom. If I want my room back, I have to sell these. There isn't enough space in my apartment for them to be out of sight, out of mind. They will be a constant reminder if I chicken out. Literal stumbling blocks.

Sitting with my back against the bed, I look around at my merchandise. This is all mine from conception to completion—my ideas, my scent formulations, my physical labor.

Few things in my life have ever happened solely because of me.

I got a business degree because my parents said it was the practical choice. Above all else, I needed to be practical. I work in property management because it's what my parents did, and they needed me when I graduated. It was only supposed to be temporary, not a career. I like my job at The Nouveau, but sometimes I feel like a part of me is withering away.

The pride I feel over these boxes of candles is gratifying, but the sense of freedom is ridiculous.

I've been telling myself it was just a hobby, but I always wanted to turn it into more. It's whimsical, which flies in the face of everything my parents drilled into me about business my whole life.

But a side hustle can be whimsical. It can be anything I want it to be.

Dec wanted to take me to dinner, but I told him I'm too busy fulfilling my promise about Bathtub Zen. His solution is to pick up food and come here. He always has a solution that leads to him getting his way.

I'm cranky, probably because I need to eat. Maybe he'll bring dessert. I could use something sweet.

When the doorbell rings, I realize I've lost track of time. I'd intended to change clothes, maybe brush my hair. But here we are.

The smell of grease and hot sauce hits me as soon as I open the door. The bags in his hand confirm it. "You got wings?"

"Hey, if I have to deliver, I'm catering to my own cravings." He walks into my apartment. "It smells like a candle shop in here."

"Well, it did before you got here. You're lucky I like wings."

He sets the bags on the kitchen counter and grabs my waist to pull me forward. "I'm lucky you like me."

I don't mean to flinch when he says it. His expression falls a little.

"If you're lucky, you remembered to get some habanero honey sauce."

"That would make me lucky, huh?"

"Well, it'll keep you from having to make a second trip."

He pulls a cup of habanero honey sauce from the bag. "I may not be good at everything, but I have a good memory."

So do I, and that's the problem. If I could turn off the memories, getting to know him again would be so much easier. The constant game of mental Whack-a-Mole sucks.

"Do you have beer?"

"Um . . ." I open the fridge. "One, and it's all yours."

"I knew I should've grabbed some."

"I have wine."

"I'll drink the beer first and see how I feel about that offer."

"Did you bring dessert?"

"I am dessert."

"I'll eat the wings first and see how I feel about that offer."

The sweet, spicy heat of the wings is comforting. They might not have been my first choice for dinner, but I have no complaints.

All I've done all day is pour and package candles. It doesn't seem like I should be this tired. I feel the way I do after a strenuous workout: happy I did the work, but glad it's over.

If this side hustle works out, I'll have a lot more pouring and packing sessions in my future. I'm sure I'll get used to it.

Using my thumb, I wipe a smear of sauce from the corner of his lips. He playfully bites at me, and I laugh as I yank my hand away from his teeth. It feels strangely natural to have him here. I'd forgotten how comfortable it was just to be with him sometimes, doing nothing special, just being together. Not every memory needs to be whacked.

I shove the empty wing bags into my trashcan. It's technically full, and I'm considering taking it out when his arms lock around me. His body is warm. A contented sigh escapes me when he kisses my neck. The trash can wait until morning.

"I changed my mind about dessert," he murmurs into my hair. "It's you."

"If I'm your dessert, then what do I get?"

"You get to come all over my face." His tongue traces the shell of my ear, and I wiggle against him. "Because that's where you'll be sitting."

Oh, damn. I haven't sat on a guy's face in a while. I love the way he lays down and buries his face between my legs, but I used to love lowering onto his face, too.

"It's been a long time since I've done that."

"You don't have to tell me."

"I meant with anyone at all."

"You've never done that with anyone else."

We both laugh. I'd prefer to think he hasn't done that with anyone else either. Pretending can be the better option sometimes. For a little while.

I let him lead me down the hall to my bedroom. We kiss like we never ended, like we've been living an epic love story all along. The truth will still be there when we're ready to confront it again.

He trips over a stack of boxes, and we fall to the bed. I laugh as he fumbles with my clothes, and then his own. Tossing the pillows aside, he lies flat on his back and motions toward his face. "Get up here, gorgeous."

Getting into position has always been the weirdest part, but I plaster on what I hope passes for a confident smile as I set my knees on either side of his head. He lifts his shoulders so I can slide my shins under them, and then he grips my hips and pulls me down. "Sit."

My glutes tighten, and I maintain a slight degree of hover. He pulls harder on my hips, forcing me to relent. To sit. It definitely feels better this way. I shake away my worry about suffocating him. He's a grown man. Stronger than me. If he needs air, he can push me up.

I know all this, but there is still a little self-consciousness lingering when his tongue runs up my seam and back again, teases around my opening before slipping inside. His fingers dig into my flesh and pull me even closer to his mouth.

He flattens his tongue and seals his lips against my tender, slick center, his teeth scraping gently as he shifts into hands-free-papaya-eating-contest mode.

My knees turn to gelatin. I couldn't hover now if I wanted to.

Dessert arrives quickly. The room spins and tiny fireworks explode up my spine. My fingers feel like they're fused to the headboard, and my knuckles are white when I attempt to open my hands. There's no strength at all left in my legs.

I'm boneless by the time he pulls me down to lie on my stomach next to him. He rolls on top of me with his legs framing mine and his erection pressed against my ass. "How do you want your legs? Like this, or do you want to spread them?"

"How do you want them?" My voice is breathy and faint.

Using his hand, he positions the crown of his cock at my pussy, dragging it through my juices a few times, moaning as he does it. "Last chance if you want to change positions."

"Take me like this."

He pushes forward. The sensation of his dick breaching my opening while he has me trapped beneath him feels so good. I know he'll still let me change if I want to, but the feeling of being overpowered and at his mercy is too fucking hot right now.

His strong upward thrusts lift my hips off the mattress as he plows into me. It's rough at a level I haven't been able to enjoy with anyone since him. I didn't realize how much I'd missed this—being used, and being able to enjoy it because I know I'm safe.

That's trust, and it's too soon to lean into that with him again. But maybe it's okay to let it be real for a little while, to just enjoy the moment. I am enjoying this moment so very much.

I feel my arousal gush around him.

"Oh, fuck yes. Squirt on my dick like a good little whore."

As if I had any choice in the matter. His grunts are deep and throaty, and I know he's seconds away from finishing.

I'm being nothing but submissive right now. He's exerting all the power physically, but I feel insanely powerful when his orgasm seizes him. The shifting dynamic of the power exchange in that tiny window of time is intoxicating. Addictive.

I lie beneath him, exhausted and happy to let sated memories surround us. Physical memories. Bodies remember in ways the mind can't suppress.

Carina

Molly doesn't even say hello before she informs me that my pressure point trick doesn't work.

"Can I set my purse down before the morning blowjob conversation begins?"

Landry turns from the coffeemaker and offers me a freshly poured cup. "It helps," she says. "The reflex won't go away completely, but it helps."

"Wait. Seriously? It doesn't work for you either?" I drop my purse onto my desk without breaking my stride.

"How well does it work for you?" She pulls the coffee cup she'd been offering out of my reach.

"Completely well." I lean forward and snag the handle. "Y'all must not be doing it right."

"I did it exactly like you said." Molly gets up from her desk and comes over to freshen up her cup.

I look around for something phallic that I don't mind sticking down my throat. There are a few breadsticks left from Friday's lunch delivery. They're stale, but it's not like I'm going to eat it. It'll actually work better in this state than if it was soft. I unroll the bag and pull one out.

"Okay. Hold this for me until I reach for it." Landry takes the hardened breadstick. "Y'all have to be missing a step."

My thumb stretches across my palm for a count of five. I fold my fingers over it and repeat the count. Then the five-second pinch, and then I reach for the stiff stick.

Tilting my head back, I open my mouth wide and prove just how far down my throat I can shove it. They both tilt their heads sideways to survey the actual depth, and their eyes widen in shock.

"You've always been able to do that," Landry says. "There's no way you used to gag, and that trick makes it go away like that."

I pull the breadstick out. "I'm telling you, it works. Get one." They each take a breadstick.

We all go through the steps together. I nod and smile to encourage them to test their results.

Molly still gags a little, but she seems happy with her progress.

Landry laughs as she pumps the breadstick as deep as she can take it.

Huh. The trick really does work better for me than it does for them. I take a few more inches before I extract it to the tip to show off.

The next thing I know, we're all huddled together in front of the coffeemaker with our heads tilted back and deep throating stale bread sticks, thrusting them faster and making obscene noises through our laughter. My eyes actually water.

But I can see clearly—or clearly enough, anyway. They're blurry through my watery vision, but there's no mistaking the two men standing transfixed just inside the office door.

Fuck!

Three women have never yanked breadsticks from their throats so fast in the history of . . . okay, fine, there's probably no recorded history of that. I throw my saliva-soaked breadstick into the trash like it's burning my hand.

Molly tosses hers into the sink.

Landry holds hers in one hand while she wipes spittle from her mouth with the other. "Hey, guys. What's up?"

Holden's cheeks are a deeper shade of red than my lipstick.

Vaughn's smile spreads slowly across his face. "Just wanted to let you know we're going off property for a while."

"Both of you?"

"Yeah. We need to go pick up some drywall. Unit 219 has wall damage that's beyond repair. The carpet's shot, too, and the carpet company can't make it out until next Friday."

"How much of the carpet needs to be replaced?"

"All of it."

"Is it pet damage?" She instinctively scrunches her nose, like she can smell the urine in the carpet.

"Some of it, but there's a burn in the shape of an iron on the bedroom floor. Stains everywhere."

I sip some coffee to soothe my throat. That breadstick may have been a bad idea. "Can't we try to clean it first?" I ask, hoping that option will sound like a good idea to Landry.

"Won't help the burn," Vaughn says.

"We could have that area patched and have the rest steam-cleaned."

He shrugs. "You could try to clean it in the living room and hall, but it has to be replaced in the bedroom. There's no way to patch a section of that carpet."

Landry sighs. "Yeah, that won't work. And if we put new carpet in the bedroom, it will make the old carpet in the hallway and living room look worse."

"But it was just installed last year." I realize how incredulous my voice sounds, but I'm not wrong. "We shouldn't have to replace it yet. A good cleaning might make it look brand new again."

"It might help, but it won't look new, and we'll lose time and money trying that." Landry shakes her head, finally throws away her breadstick. "I'd rather replace it and get it ready for a new tenant as soon as possible."

Holden hasn't looked up from his shoes since this conversation began. He's shifting his weight from one foot to the other. Poor guy. He probably won't be able to make eye contact with any of us for a month.

"Do you have anything else to add?" Landry asks. Her voice cuts sharper than usual. She's agitated with me for arguing about the carpet. I understand why she would be, but I'm still not sure the carpet really needs to be replaced.

This is ridiculous. Why am I doing this? I don't want to be the manager, so there's no reason for me to questioning her decisions. She knows how to work within a budget.

"No. Sorry. It's just force of habit to analyze costs."

"No harm in weighing all the options," Landry says, her voice already softening.

"Do y'all need anything while we're out?" Vaughn asks. "More breadsticks?"

"Go!" Landry says.

Holden snickers without lifting his head.

The three of us wait until they leave the office to laugh.

"Wow, eventful morning so far," I say.

And then my mother walks in.

Declan

THIS IS THE SECOND time this week I've pulled into a parking spot with no memory of driving there. In my defense, Rina activated every carnal memory we ever shared Sunday night, and they're still playing like movie clips in my head. On a loop.

She put a fucking spell on me or something. I can't get her out of my head, not even for a minute. On the bright side, an early morning meeting with my CPA has never been so enjoyable. He was spitting numbers and advice, but I was tasting her on my tongue and seeing into a future that didn't have a damn thing to do with my bottom line.

The shine of her hair and softness of her skin means a hell of a lot more right now than diversifying investments and increasing capital.

I've never not been able to flip the switch and turn off everything else when the time came to focus on business, but the switch ain't switching right now. I think I'm permanently turned on.

A session with my chiropractor might be just what I need. If Dorian can't bring me crashing back into reality, nothing can. The receptionist smiles and buzzes me through the inner door so I can change clothes.

"I have breaking news," I say with more enthusiasm than I intended as I climb onto the table.

"Shock me."

"I went back to that hot yoga class."

"It doesn't have to be hot yoga. You don't have to torture yourself."

"If you repeat this, I'll call you a liar, but I like it."

"That tracks. You probably don't believe in the validity of anything that doesn't include some level of physical discomfort."

"Pain leads to growth."

"Okay, tough guy. How often are you going to classes?"

"I went two weeks in a row."

"How many days of the week?"

"Baby steps."

"You've got to go more often than once a week. Let's shoot for at least three, okay?"

"Instead of coming here?"

"Nice try. In addition to, but you already knew that."

"When am I supposed to run my business? I can't spend all my days here or in a yoga class."

"Do you think those other people in class don't have busy lives and responsibilities? Find a way. You only get one body. Nobody else is going to take care of it for you."

My smile is involuntary. All I can think of is the ways Rina takes care of my body.

"Whoever she is, maybe she'd be willing to go to hot yoga with you."

Dammit. I hate being the obvious sap who can't wipe the silly-ass smile off his face because of some woman. But she's not just some woman. My spine cracks, and the tension in my lower back dissolves like sugar in hot water.

"She prefers some kind of *tonga* class. Or flow."

"Maybe you might like a *tonga* class, too." She helps me off the table as she mocks me. "If you gave it a chance."

"No, I don't think so. I tried the flow version. All I liked about it was watching her flow from one position to the next. I don't flow well."

"I don't doubt that, but it couldn't have been all bad. You obviously met someone there."

"I knew her before, just ran into her there."

"Keep going to yoga. Like you said, what woman wants a man with a back injury?"

"Ah, come on. She might want him if he's working on healing it."

"Exactly. So keep working on it."

I missed a text from Tess during my appointment.

Should I send something to The Nouveau today? It's been a while since you've sent them a gift.

They're good.

That's why you should send them a gift.

Haha. Get back to work.

Why'd it take you so long to respond?

I was in a meeting.

There's no meeting on your schedule.

It was unscheduled.

Anything I need to follow up on?

Follow up on some past-due invoices.

I've already yelled at all those people today. I need to be nice to someone now.

Call your wife. Send her a gift.

Spontaneous gifts make her suspicious. She has trust issues.

Send them more often and she won't.

You are the last person I'd take relationship advice from.

I give great advice.

Take it yourself. Be safe.

Thanks.

She's probably right about Rina deserving a gift, but not something sent to the whole office. I should get her something personal, something meaningful. This is the type of thing I normally have Tess handle, which I guess makes it a lot less personal and meaningful.

Shit. She's right. No one should take relationship advice from me.

I'll come up with a gift she deserves. It might take me a while, but I'll figure it out. I'm not completely inept at relationships, just rusty.

Carina

Landry's been a little standoffish since my mom showed up unannounced on Monday. I'd just made an issue of putting new carpet in a make-ready, and then my mother showed up fresh from a Houston Multi-Unit Rental Association meeting and started dropping loaded comments about the economy and falling occupancy predictions, constantly casting her wary eyes in my direction as if she were cueing me to weigh in and support her concerns. To choose sides.

I hate that I felt even an ounce of betrayal for not doing what she wanted, but years of programming don't disappear just because you insert a few degrees of separation.

I'd never spy on Landry, but even I have to admit it didn't look great. My mother couldn't be discreet if she tried.

Landy's always careful not to say anything negative about my parents. I know they piss her off sometimes, but she keeps it professional. I'm sure she vents to Vaughn about them, but she's never once slipped up and said anything disparaging about them to me.

Frankly, I think my mom could take a lesson or two in business decorum from Landry. Her head would spin if she knew I felt that way. She prides herself on being the epitome of a successful businesswoman, but there's a thin veil between being cunning and being a cunt.

There's a new episode of *The Rest of the Story* tonight, but Landry hasn't invited me to stay and watch it with her.

I scroll on my phone for a few minutes, and then I pretend to be shocked by something on my screen. "Oh, wow. I forgot there was a new episode tonight. Do you want to come to my place and watch it?"

"Oh . . ." she falters. "Um, I totally forgot, too. But I bought snacks. And wine. I meant to ask you, but I guess I just assumed you'd come up after work. This week has been crazy."

"It really has," I agree, suddenly realizing that we're talking about this right in front of Molly, and we've never invited her to watch the show with us. I turn toward her and try to sound casual. "Do you watch it?"

"No. I don't like reality TV."

My sigh of relief is probably more obvious than I want it to be, but Molly doesn't seem offended. Landry is watching me for an answer. "I'd love to come up and watch it together. It would honestly feel weird to watch it alone at this point."

"Right? I'd probably end up calling you to talk about it the whole time, anyway." She laughs.

The day drags until Vonnie shows up mid-afternoon with Lolita strapped across her chest in a baby sling. The snake's head is out, her tongue flicking at the air.

"Is she sick?" I ask.

"No, just something new I'm testing out to keep her contained when we're strolling around. Truth be told, I don't think she likes it much. She keeps trying to climb out of it."

She lifts Lolita from the fabric and holds her out to me. In my peripheral vision, I see Landry shudder as I let the snake wrap around my arm. Her bright red and orange skin still fascinates me. She hardly looks real sometimes.

Vonnie sheds the sling and takes Lolita back, letting her wind around her waist the way she usually does. "Here you go, Lollie Girl. I should've known you wouldn't like that damn thing. You need to be free, like me."

"Like mother, like daughter," Landry teases.

"Hey, hon, I should probably tell you something." Vonnie rubs Lolita's head on her cheek in a show of affection. "It's not a big deal or anything, but she might mention it."

We all stop and stare. There's rarely a hint of trepidation in Vonnie's voice, but she definitely sounds like she's proceeding with caution here.

"Go on," Landry says.

"I ran into that woman from 501 in the elevator earlier today, and she wouldn't shut up about how our Vaughn has been showing her so much extra attention lately. You know how she does. Anyway, I had my fill of her stupid shit, so I told her it's natural for men to flirt a little more than usual right before they get married, but it doesn't mean anything, so she should take a cold shower and get over herself."

I giggle at her use of *our Vaughn*.

Landry blinks in rapid succession for a few seconds. "You told her Vaughn was getting married?"

"More like implied it."

"Whom did you imply he was marrying?"

"Don't worry. I clarified that. She tried to play dumb, but I made damn sure she knew he was marrying you. As if she didn't already know. Ooooh, she makes me so mad."

"You can't tell people things like that!"

"Well, it was that or knock her ass out. I had to shut her up somehow."

"Knock her out next time!"

Molly and I crack up.

Landry is not laughing.

Our Vaughn walks in just in time to hear her say, "What if she tells the entire building that Vaughn and I are getting married?"

"We are?"

I didn't know his eyebrows could arch that high.

"That's what Vonnie told 501."

"Huh, I should've thought of that. Thanks, Vonnie." He walks past us to check out the snacks in our kitchenette along the back wall. "I wonder if it'll actually discourage her."

Landry stares at his back with her mouth agape.

Vonnie shrugs. "I did what I could, darlin'."

"Do I at least get a ring out of this charade?" Landry's voice is heavy with sarcasm, but Vaughn kisses the top of her head as he walks past her desk with a handful of mini peanut butter cups on his way out. "You got it, Princess."

Something in his voice makes my inner romance girlie giddy. I'm not entirely sure he was kidding. I can't pinpoint why, but if he buys her a ring in the immediate future, it won't surprise me.

Now, if she actually agrees to wear it? Break out the smelling salts because I'll faint on the spot. Landry's been married, and she's not a fan of the concept.

Vaughn is leaving Landry's apartment when I approach her door. He holds it open for me. "Enjoy your trash TV show." He smiles and shakes his head.

"I plan to enjoy every minute. Thanks!"

Landry's face lights up from the kitchen when she sees me walk in. "I have something to show you!"

I freeze. If there is a ring on her finger . . .

She holds up two champagne flutes. "Aren't these cute? I couldn't resist buying them but I haven't had an occasion to use them yet. Tonight is the perfect time to break them in."

They're cute, but in the most kitschy, obnoxious way possible. The stems are Rosie the Riveter, but she's dressed all in sparkly pink from her jeans to her bandana. Girl power but make it girlie-girl power. Totally Landry.

Honestly, I think I'd have hated them in the store, but seeing them here in her hands, they're perfect.

The Rest of the Story doesn't vote people off the island. It's not an elimination show, but three have already gone home, sent packing by their own egos. The remaining three now have to handle the anthology. They've agreed on a charity, and tonight is the cover reveal. I don't know how they're going to get enough stories to fill it. Maybe they'll extend the show so they have time to write more?

These three women actually get along well now. Maybe they've grown; maybe they've just bonded over their dislike of the other three who've left. The show has become a much tamer version of what we saw in previews and in the early episodes. I guess it's nice that they've learned to work together, but it's getting boring. Where's the drama?

A limo comes into view from the left side of the shot, slowly rolling up the long narrow driveway to the luxury cabin.

We both sit straight up. "Oh, shit," Landry says. "Who's coming back?"

"What if it's all three of them?"

Leaning forward, we watch as the car door opens and a red stiletto heel emerges. The scene cuts to a tall, elegant woman striding up to the porch in her red heels with a man in a black suit at her side. Her dark hair is perfectly swirled into a tight bun. Her dress is black to match the man's suit, and her fingernails match the red of her shoes.

She looks important, but I don't recognize her or the man walking next to her. "Who are they?"

"Maybe they're the producers?"

"What are they going to do? Cancel the show in front of the cameras?"

"That would be dramatic."

"True."

The author who said she owned kissing in the rain opens the door. She looks stunned at their appearances. They're obviously not lost travelers. The duo enters the cabin without waiting for an invitation.

Miss Trademarked Eyes bounds down the stairs with her phone in her hand. She stops short at the bottom when she sees their visitors.

Before anyone can begin the introductions, there is another knock at the door.

Their limo driver has unloaded luggage and brought it all up the steps to the porch. He doesn't await instructions once the front door is open. As if he's been there before, he pulls all the Luis Vuitton pieces toward an empty bedroom, returns and takes all the black bags to another.

The three remaining authors all have upstairs rooms. And they obviously have new housemates, who will be staying downstairs. The trio looks frantically back and forth between each other as if one of them must know what's happening.

"I'm sure you're wondering who we are and why we're here," the man says.

A chair scrapes against the floor as the new woman pulls it away from the dining table. She sits with her hands folded on the tabletop, her neck long and regal as she prepares to be formally introduced.

"This is the publisher for the anthology you've been working on, Madelyn Woodvale. And I'm your editor, Lars Bennington. We'll be taking over the administrative tasks, freeing you up to work on writing your stories."

"Publisher?"

"Editor?"

"Um, we weren't aware the show was sending an editor. We don't have stories ready for you yet, so there's really no need for you to be here."

"And we'll be publishing it ourselves."

Condescension drips from Madelyn Woodvale's laughter. "No, you will not. The anthology is being traditionally published. We are here to make sure you meet the editorial deadlines, and to give viewers a peek at what goes into creating a book."

"Yes," Lars agrees. "And we already have a backlog of outside submissions to read and consider while we wait for yours, so don't worry about us. We have plenty to keep busy."

"So, if you're the publisher, who are we to this project?"

Lars clears his throat. "Presumably, you're writers."

"But we have no creative control over the anthology?"

"We're fucking minions?" Miss Trademarked Eyes looks like hers are about to pop right out of her head.

As reality dawns for the three authors, their nostrils flare and their cheeks flush.

They've spent weeks arguing about the cover, the formatting, the number of stories needed, the order of their stories . . . doing pretty much everything except writing their stories, which, as it turns out, is their only role.

"Damn." I refill my wine. "What do you think the odds are they all walk out?"

Landry holds her glass out so I can refill hers, too. "Oh, Kissing in the Rain will be gone by morning, but I think she'll sneak out alone in the middle of the night."

"Is it weird that I feel bad for them?" I take a gulp from my wine glass. "It was sort of their thing, you know? They were doing all this work, and to have someone swoop in and take it away, that's gotta hurt."

"But in reality, it was never really theirs. The network came up with the idea. And they didn't actually say the authors would have creative control. Everyone just assumed that was the deal, including the audience."

"Lies of omission are still deceptions."

"But the shocking surprises and power grabs are the best part of reality TV. People being kind to each other is only entertaining in baking competitions."

"You're not wrong, but it feels so mean."

"Being mean is how these people got on this show to begin with."

"I know." I swirl my wine and think about the boxes stacked in my bedroom. If someone stole Bathtub Zen right out from under me, I'd be devastated. I know it's not the same, but I can't help but empathize with these authors. It's crazy because I don't even like these women. But I might like Madelyn and Lars even less.

I look at Madelyn sitting with her ankles crossed and her thin lips pulled into a tight smile that's about as friendly as a piranha, and I see my mother in that chair. Well, this show just messed me up in ways I was entirely unprepared for. No way I'm missing an episode now.

Good job, showrunner. Good fucking job. You got me.

"Are you okay?" Landry pauses the show.

"Yeah, I'm good."

"No, you're not."

"Madelyn reminds me of my mom."

"Oh. Yeah, I can see that. Do you want to stop watching it?"

"Don't even think about turning it off."

We laugh, but I do it to hold back the sizzling urge to share Bathtub Zen with her. I don't know why I'm suddenly bursting with the need to tell her. But if I'm going to make it official, keeping it a secret seems wrong. Deceptive.

I know she'll be supportive. It's not like I'm going to quit my job to sell candles and bath products, but the niggling fear of being judged is in my DNA.

"I get that it's hard to talk about your parents, especially with me, since I work for them, but I'm here if you ever want to. If you ever just need someone to listen, I will."

She's a better friend than I've ever had. My mom micromanaged my friendship choices until I left for college. The best thing about being away at school was being able to choose my own friends, not that I had any idea how to navigate friendships. I had a boatload of trust issues and social awkwardness, but at least I got to choose who I unleashed it on.

"So, I have a confession."

She leans forward. "Yeah?"

"I have this passion project I've been keeping a secret." Wow, that was so easy. I just opened my mouth and let it out.

"What? Tell me everything. You're opening your own yoga studio, aren't you?"

"No. I'm not even an instructor."

"You're becoming an instructor!"

"No. It doesn't have anything to do with yoga." I take a deep breath. "Well, the name sort of does. And the logo. It's candles and stuff."

"You have a business name and a logo? Do you have a website?"

"Not yet. I'm going to start it in person. At farmers markets and maybe in some shops that take merch on consignment."

"When do I get to see your products?"

"I can bring some into the office to show you."

"You better! That's so cool, Carina. How long have you been working on it?"

"An embarrassingly long time. I was afraid to commit to it until recently." I take a sip of my wine. "Declan encouraged me to go for it."

"I knew I liked him from the moment we met."

"What farmers market are you selling at?"

"I'm still waiting to hear back from one. Nothing is official yet."

"It will be. I'm going to come take pictures of you being mobbed by customers. You can put them on your website."

"The website I don't have yet."

"Yet is the keyword. You will. What's your company name?"

"Bathtub Zen."

"Yes! Perfection." She lifts her glass to toast, and I clink mine against it.

"We can finish watching the show now," I say.

"Whatever you say, boss babe."

"You're *my* boss."

"Only here. You're about to be your own boss out there." She jerks her head toward the window. It's a clear night, and the moon is full. She lives on the eighth floor, and I can see an airplane in the distance. It's still climbing to its cruising altitude, on the way to some unknown destination. It leaves me feeling wistful.

Landry restarts the TV, but I stare out the window for a few more seconds. My life has gone a little off course, but it's all just minor changes. Declan is back in my life, and I'm about to launch a company selling candles with cheeky labels and fizzy bath bombs.

Somehow, I've manifested my mother's worst fears for me without even trying: a totally impractical business venture and a boyfriend who cares more about using the right fertilizer than the right fork for a salad.

Boyfriend.

I guess it's the right word, but it's still a shock to my psyche when it pops into my head so effortlessly. It's time to admit it. I have a boyfriend.

And his big truck isn't even compensating for anything.

Lucky me.

Declan

TESS SENDS ME A text telling me to come out of my office and look at something. Her desk is close enough to my door that she could've just yelled for me, but no, she has to send a message that I have to take the time to read and now have to delete. So many extra steps.

"What?" I ask, holding my door open.

"Come over here. I want you to look at this."

"It's a toy. Are you trying to tell me you're having a kid?"

"Guess again."

"You're adopting a kid?"

"No kids are involved! It's a plush animal to represent the real endangered animal you can adopt. Look how cute the red panda is!"

"Are you trying to get me to make a donation so you can have that toy?"

She sighs like I'm the one who's being difficult. "It's for Carina. You can make a donation in her name to help save an endangered animal and she'll get this little guy as a keepsake."

"That's fucking weird."

"It's thoughtful. You can tell her you saw the opportunity, and it made you think of her."

"Telling someone a lie is your idea of being thoughtful?"

"Well, it's not a total lie. I saw the opportunity, and then I called you out here to point out that it probably reminds you of her. And now that I've mentioned it, it does, doesn't it?"

"No. Not at all."

"Okay, what about the blue-footed booby? Look how cute that is!"

"Just when I thought this couldn't get any weirder." I turn to go back to my office.

"At least come look at the river otter."

"I am not giving her a toy otter. Order it for your wife, who deserves a medal for staying married to you, by the way."

"I'm right about this, Declan."

I pause at the threshold of my office. "That otter better not show up at The Nouveau, Tess. I'm serious. Do not."

"They have wildlife nesting dolls!"

"She is a grown-ass woman. I'm not buying her a toy."

Unless it's a toy made for a grown-ass woman. Hmm, that's not a bad idea . . .

"I'm going to be out for the rest of the afternoon."

"Don't buy her a sex toy, Declan. Unless you're taking her to the store with you. Women really prefer to pick those out for themselves."

"Who said anything about a damn sex toy?"

"That shit-eating grin on your face said it."

"If you're just dying to buy something online, order some more water bottles. I can pick out my own gifts."

"Since when?"

"One day, you're going to go too far, and I'm going to fire you."

"And the next day, you'll call me and beg me to come back."

Her ability to make me laugh is her job security. It doesn't hurt that she's like the sister I never had. She knows we work together too damn well for me to fire her. Maybe I'll make a donation and get her the otter.

But I'm getting Carina something else entirely.

I hadn't planned on buying something this big, but the more I looked around, the more I realized every toy in the store was just a different version of the same three or four devices. She has a drawer full of toys, but as soon as I saw the cushions, I knew we'd get more use of out of those. The positions I imagined the moment I spotted the ramp and wedge combo . . . these things sold themselves.

Their discreet giftwrapping may not have the store name printed on it, but I'm pretty sure this red and black foiled paper is recognizable to anyone who's shopped there. It matches their shopping bags. The text from their logo is the only part that's missing. The embossed pomegranate is all over the paper.

I swear every person I pass on the sidewalk smirks when they see it. The woman who stopped to watch me wrestle it out of my truck smiled and nodded. Nosy neighbors all over the place. I should've wrapped it in a plain black trash bag.

Carina takes one look at it when she opens her door, and she says, "Ohhhh, okay." Then she burst into laughter. "What do they sell that is that big?"

"Can I bring it inside, please?"

"Sure."

She gestures to her dining table to suggest I set it there.

"Do you want to open it before we leave or after we get back?"

"That depends. If I open it now, will we still make it to yoga?"

"No guarantees."

"I have to know what this is." She pulls on one side of the paper until the top pops loose, and then she turns it to do the same on the other end.

I forgot how long it takes her to open presents. She never tears the paper if she can help it. "Are you really going to reuse that paper?" I ask.

"You're right." She rips a strip that exposes the top. "It's a mat?"

"Keep going."

When she has it fully unwrapped, she steps back and looks at it from various angles. "Wow. No one has ever bought me sex furniture before."

"It's not exactly furniture."

She reaches for the brochure that's attached by a plastic thread and flips through it. "So many options."

"Should we break them in?"

"I think we better go to yoga first. Some of these positions look like I need to stretch before we try them."

I toss the wedges onto the floor. They're connected with Velcro strips, and they land exactly the way they'd been displayed in the store. "I bet I could stretch you well enough."

Her lashes flutter, but she smiles as she's rolling her eyes. And then she drops to her knees and drapes herself over the ramp cushion with her ass up and her head down on the smaller wedge piece attached to the narrow end. "This is the perfect height. It's comfy."

"Good to know." I adjust my dick in my shorts. Yoga is canceled.

She flips over with her hips at the top of the ramp and her shoulders down on the lower pieces. "I bet there are a few ways this angle could be useful."

"I'm thinking of a few right now."

I reach for my waistband, but she pops back up to standing like she's on a spring. "Let's go get all sweaty and limber."

"We could do that here."

"But first, we're going to yoga."

I reluctantly follow her to the door, but I steal a kiss before we step outside. She ends it way sooner than I want. My groan of disappointment fills her apartment. Her playful laugh leads us outside.

My balance has improved so much since my first class, but I'll be lucky if I don't break my neck tonight. We're going to have to put our mats in opposite corners of the room. And I'm going to have to keep my eyes far from her body, especially once we move to the floor exercises.

I already can't get the image of her on the floor with her body so perfectly propped out of my head.

One glimpse of her in rabbit pose and I'll have to leave the room before class ends for the first time, and it won't be because of the heat.

She insists on showering alone when we get back to her place. I raid her snacks. If I can't join her in the shower, I'm for sure wiping out her chocolate-covered pretzels.

The air-conditioner blows from the vent right above me, and when it hits my sweat-soaked shorts and tank top, I decide I'd be better off naked.

There's a knock on her door.

Shit. That's unfortunate timing. Maybe they'll go away.

I stack the last three pretzels and shove them into my mouth.

They knock again. I ignore it and continue to chew. It's probably a neighbor who wants to borrow something. She's friendly with everybody who lives here, but tonight, they can go mooch off someone else. We've got plans.

A third round of knocking starts up. And then the doorknob turns. *What the hell?* And then a voice sings out, "Helllooo. I know you're home. Your car's here. I was in the neighborhood and I—"

I've never actually met the woman, but I don't need to be told I'm looking at Angela Melendez. Carina's mom. In the flesh. Not as much flesh as I'm showing, but . . .

Carina comes down the hall wearing a towel and using another to dry her hair, blocking her face. "Shower's all yours," she says, flipping her head back, causing the towel to fall away from her face. She sees her mother now, too.

I cough, and a cloud of pretzel dust leaves my mouth.

Her mother's eyes map the coordinates of everything in her field of vision: her daughter in a towel, me standing naked in the kitchen, and sex cushions on the floor amidst a pile of highly recognizable wrapping paper. If you've driven in this town, you've seen the store's billboards often enough to recognize it, whether you've shopped there or not.

"Those are for yoga!" Carina blurts, pulling her shoulders back, which causes her towel to hit the floor.

My teeth bear down on my bottom lip, but it's no use. Really? Like those cushions are more conspicuous than my dick? I fucking lose it.

Now we're both naked in front of her mother, who appears frozen in place. And I'm apparently the only one who finds it amusing.

"Can you toss me one of those towels, babe?"

"Oh. Yeah. Right." She throws the one in her hand at me and squats down to retrieve the one at her feet. We wrap ourselves as her mother stares into the middle distance between us. I watch as Carina pulls her shoulders back again, but not defensively this time.

She goes from shocked and panicked to calm, cool, and collected in one breath. "Mom, you remember Declan, right? We go to the same yoga studio now. Small world, huh?"

Her mother's disapproving glare turns to ice at the mention of my name. "Was slumming it with him once not enough?"

"Seriously? You just saw him naked. I can't imagine that's really a question at this point."

The instinct to defend myself from her mother's comment about slumming it rises, but Carina carries on. "He was never beneath me, but he owns his own company now, and he's doing quite well. You want to know something, though? If he were still pushing a lawn mower for someone else, I'd date him again, anyway."

"We raised you to respect yourself more than this."

"I couldn't respect my current life choices more if I tried. But you need to learn some respect. Don't ever barge into my apartment like this again."

"No one answered when I knocked. I was worried about you."

"Why are you here in the first place? You never drop by unannounced."

"I was in the neighborhood and thought maybe we could go to dinner."

"You schedule dinners. Spontaneity is a foreign language for you."

Her mother pulls her phone from her purse. "If I have to schedule dinner with my daughter, so be it. What day works for you?"

"Next Wednesday."

They exchange dueling glares, but her mother gives in first. "Fine. I've put you on my calendar. I'll be in touch beforehand to firm up the details."

"Perfect."

Her mother turns on her heels, casts one last glance at the cushions, and lets herself out.

"It was nice to finally meet you," I call after her.

She screams in frustration on the other side of the door before her heels click-clack down the stairs.

Carina stares at the door. I have to remind myself that miserable woman is still her mom, no matter what.

"Well, now you've stood up to her twice."

She laughs a little, but she's angry and sad, and I know this is hard for her. "Why didn't you just open the door when she knocked?"

I look down. "I wasn't exactly dressed for company."

"Right. I'm sorry."

"Don't apologize. I understand."

"I know we both had expectations for tonight, but—"

"You don't have to explain. Is it okay if I grab a shower and stay for a while, anyway?"

"Yeah. Pizza?"

"Only because you're out of pretzels."

The pizza is technically burned, but we eat it anyway. She falls asleep on my shoulder, and I carry her to bed, crawl in next to her, and wish I could give her an easier relationship with her parents.

Having me in her life is only going to make it harder, but I'm not going anywhere.

I'll fight for her this time, even if it means I have to battle my pride and learn to deal with her parents.

Carina

"You really didn't have to get up early on a Saturday to help me set up." I offer Landry the last donut hole in the bag we've been snacking from. Vendors are still unloading at their booths, but soon, shoppers will start wandering through. It still seems surreal that I'm doing this. "But thank you for being here."

"I wouldn't have missed the chance to support you on your first day."

"It's so much more work to get set up than I realized. If I don't sell anything, I'll probably just give everything away so I don't have to repack it all." I laugh because I'm joking about giving things away, of course, but I'm not looking forward to packing all this stuff back up at closing time.

"You are going to sell out. Positive thoughts only."

My coffee is still hot enough to burn my tongue, which seems impossible because it feels like we've already been here all day. Cars and trucks pull away from booths. We're close to opening time. My car's in the lot. I didn't realize I could've driven all the way in to unload, so I made four trips using the hand truck I borrowed from The Nouveau. It's okay, though. It helped burn off some of my nervous energy. But I'm glad I trusted Vaughn's advice and didn't try to do it without the hand truck.

Someone rings a bell, which feels ominous because it sounds like the start of a boxing match. Customers don't stampede, but a steady stream flows through the gates. They splinter off and head in different directions once they're inside.

It's obvious some of these people are regulars, and they're going straight for their favorite vendors. I'm in a good spot, right between a woman selling handmade body jewelry and a pair of women selling everything from knit beanies to crocheted penises in various sizes and colors.

Nothing too wholesome about my neighbors here, thankfully. And we're not next to crates full of cabbages, so there's that to be thankful for.

I like being nestled between these women—not only are they experienced sellers, they're funny. I've laughed at their banter while I set up, and they've both come over and complimented the quotes I used on my candle labels and the scents of my bath products. They like my logo and my company name, too. Positive feedback from Declan and Landry is great, but to hear it from strangers puts a little extra steel in my courage.

The body jewelry table draws a pretty young crowd, but my neighbor on the other side doesn't cover her penises, so I don't hide my pussy quote labels. Or the dildo ones. Or the Declan quote about the lack of peace in his aura. I smile, remembering him saying that. He was so close to getting it right, and yet so far from it.

One of the young shoppers calls her mom over to show her something. The woman browses my merchandise while her daughter and friend debate whether she should get the lip ring with her birthstone or the blue crystal that matches her eyes. "Why don't your bath products have funny sayings on the packaging as well?" she asks me.

"Oh. I never thought about doing that."

"You should. It would make your branding more consistent."

"Thanks. That's a good idea. I don't know why it never occurred to me."

"There's a lot to think about when you're launching a brand. It can get overwhelming." She picks up my candle that clarifies the lack of dildo serial killers and says, "I need this for my office."

"Do you work for an adult novelty company?" I'm trying to keep it PG because of the kids.

"No. I'm a serial killer."

I pause for way too long to play it off and pretend she didn't shock me. Landry snorts cold brew out her nose. We all get a good laugh at my expense, but I get a sale out of it, so I don't mind.

"Ma'am, I'm going to need to see your ID. I heard you're breaking some decency laws over here." Declan's deep voice cuts through the murmur of shoppers. Every woman within earshot giggles. He hands me a fresh coffee.

More caffeine is probably not a good idea, but I'm weak in the face of temptation. And when it comes to the coffee, too.

He picks up a candle and reads the label aloud. "There is not enough peace in my aura to let that shit go." He eyes me accusingly. "Huh, I wonder how you came up with that."

"Being quoted on a Bathtub Zen label is the highest form of flattery."

"What's my cut?"

"I think you know the answer to that."

"Tess would get a kick out of it. I'll buy her one."

"You don't have to pay for it. Consider it compensation for my exploitation of your wisdom."

He tosses twenty-five dollars on the table, anyway. And then he brings the candle to his nose and inhales before loudly announcing, "Damn, this candle smells amazing!"

A few people come over to see what he's talking about. His smile is pompous, but well-earned, as I greet my new potential customers. He definitely drew them over here.

Landry pulls a small notebook from her purse and says, "She's running a contest for witty slogans to go on her bath products. You can write suggestions here with your email address or phone number. If she uses your quote, you'll get a free product."

I can't believe she just told someone that.

The next thing I know, she's standing in front of my table, telling anyone who will pay attention to her. Declan is shoving a candle under the nose of every woman who stands still long enough—and he's shamelessly flirting to get them to stand still a little longer. My own guerilla marketing team.

I'm not sure what my sales would've looked like without the help of Landry and Dec, but by the end of the day, I only have enough items remaining to repack one container. I did well. Surprisingly well.

I'd like to sleep for the rest of the weekend, but I have to create new merchandise because I booked this table every Saturday for the next three months.

"Let's go celebrate." Declan closes my trunk and wraps his arms around me.

I yawn. "Sorry. That's not in response to your offer, I promise. I'm just exhausted."

"We'll go to dinner, and then I'll tuck you in safe and sound."

"And alone?"

"I don't think you should be alone after such a strenuous day. You probably need someone close in case you need something."

"You should've been a nurse," I tease.

"Are you saying you want to play doctor? Because that's what I heard."

"Listen, doc, you gotta buy me dinner first."

"How about dinner and drinks?"

"That might be the perfect prescription for what ails me."

"I'm very good at my job."

"Doctor of the year."

"Wait till you hear what your copay is."

"As long as you keep making house calls, it's worth it."

I follow him out of the lot to drop my car off at my place. When I hop up into his truck, I'm already feeling re-energized. "It smells good in here."

"Smells like this sexy candlemaker I know."

Declan

I WANT TO TAKE her back to my place after dinner. But the sex wedges are at her place, and breaking those in is totally worth an extra ten minutes on the drive home.

"You were a definite hit at the farmers market," she says, kicking off her shoes inside her door.

"Your products were a hit."

"If I place them in shops on consignment, can I assign you shifts to go flirt with shoppers there, too?"

"Flirt? Me? I don't know what you're talking about."

She pops the lid off the tub with her leftover merchandise. "Do you prefer lavender and mint or orange blossom and sandalwood?"

"If you're trying to pay me in products, I had something else in mind."

"I'm asking what scent you'd prefer in our bath. I need a hot bath, and you're here, so it would be bad manners not to invite you to join me."

"I like what you like."

"Lavender-mint then." She reaches into the tub and takes out a bag and a couple of bath bombs. "Hope you like your bath extra fizzy."

"As long as you're in it."

By the time she pours in half a bag of bath salts and drops in both bath bombs, the scent makes my eyes water. And she wasn't kidding about wanting it hot. The mirror fogs before the tub's halfway full, and there is steam rising from the water.

But when she lowers herself to sit between my legs, it's perfect. She leans back against my chest and I scoop water in my hands and pour it over her breasts, watching it bead as it trickles across her skin.

"Mmmm." Her head lolls on my shoulder, and her hands rest on my knees, sticking up out of the water like mountains. This tub's not big enough for two adults to bathe in, but her nipples are taut under my fingers and she's not pushing my hands away, so it's the perfect size for us right now.

The oils from her products make our bodies slick. The frictionless glide of skin on skin is sensual. There's a soft sheen on her tits when my hands move across them. It's beautiful, but I can't leave her uncovered for long. They feel too good. All of her feels amazing.

"How's your back?" she asks.

"Not as good as your front."

She dips her hand into the water to splash at me. "This is nice."

"So nice."

"I could fall asleep right here."

I pinch her nipple to make sure she doesn't. She splashes me again.

"As good as this bath feels, we should get out soon," I say. "Move to your bed, where I can get some traction."

"I might fall asleep on you there, too."

"You won't."

She laughs as she stands to grab a towel. My eyes roam up her wet body.

I lean forward and open the drain before I get out. Water gurgles into the pipes, and the condensation on the mirror morphs from a blanket of steam into individual water droplets that break apart and roll down the surface.

Droplets run down her neck, too. Damn, she looks good in a towel, but I can't wait to see her bare body draped over those wedges. Even after she's dry, her skin still shines from the oils in our bath.

I get the wedges from her closet.

"How'd you know that's where they were?" she asks.

"Seemed like the most logical place."

"Did you just call me the most logical? Hold on. Let me get my phone so you can say it again."

I toss the wedges onto the bed, and then I pick her up and toss her next to them. Her towel flies open when she lands, and I drop mine and join her.

Our skin still slides together easily when I tangle my legs with hers. Her kiss is warm and eager. When I pull the wedges closer, she lifts her hips so I can slide them under her. The smaller cushion supports her at the perfectly elevated height to go deep without such an upward thrust.

She moans so sweetly when I push into her. When her walls pulse around me, I know the angle is good for her, too.

Her fingers circling her clit while I fuck her is one of my favorite sights, and when her breath hitches and her hips jerk, mine do the same.

Holding out until she comes is hard, but worth it when her pussy clamps like a vise on my dick. There was no dirty talk, no teasing tonight. No words at all.

Until she falls asleep on my chest and I whisper, "I love you," knowing she won't hear it, but needing to say it, anyway.

Her rhythmic breathing halts for a moment.

Is she holding her breath? Did she hear me?

She doesn't open her eyes. Doesn't say it back. Her breathing resumes the cadence of sleep.

Carina

"I HOPE VONNIE STOPS in today," I say as I set my purse on my desk. "She inspired my new candle, and I brought her one."

Landry steps closer to read the label. "Buy another box of wine and let that shit go." She laughs and nods her head in approval. "That's a good one. I hope you made a lot of those."

"My aunt and uncle own a wine shop in The Woodlands," Molly says. "I bet they'd take some of those."

"How fancy is their wine shop? You don't think having the word box on the label instead of bottle will offend them?"

"Oh, there's fancy wine in boxes now. Trust me. But you could always do some labels that say box and some that say bottle."

The inspiration was Vonnie wanting us to get a box of rosé, but I can see how having both might increase my sales chances.

"That's a good idea," Landry says. "Do both."

"It's unanimous. I'm sold. I'll make the new labels tonight."

"How's it going with Declan?" Landry asks. "You haven't mentioned him much lately."

"Things are good. The same. You know. Nothing new."

I'm still not sure if I dreamed he told me he loved me or if it really happened. He hasn't said it since I woke up confused about it, so I'm pretty sure I dreamed it. It's not like I can ask him to confirm if he said it. What if he didn't? Then I look like I want him to say it. But if he did, I have to know if I'm ready to say it back.

It was definitely a dream.

Autry McDaniel comes in holding a little white surprise. And it's not a box of donuts.

"That is the cutest dog I've ever seen!" Landry bounces on her toes, already reaching out to hold it. "Is a little boy or a girl?"

"This is Walter. Named after Walter Cronkite, of course."

Sure. Who wouldn't have known that?

He gingerly passes the little dog to Landry. "Now, I know I should've amended my lease and paid my pet deposit before I brought him home, but I just couldn't leave him. He chose me." His eyes get a little misty.

Well, damn. This is the sweetest thing I never expected to see.

"It's fine," Landry says, cooing at the puppy. "How big will he get?"

"They say he's a teacup, so not much bigger than he is right now."

"Oh, you got purse dog," Molly says. "So cute!"

Autry clears his throat. "I won't be putting Walter into a purse, but he is cute, isn't he?"

"He's adorable." I can't resist going over to pet him. "We'll get the pet clause added to your lease later today. Don't worry about it, Autry."

Vonnie comes into the office as Autry takes Walter back from Landry. The tiny dog settles against his shoulder like he already knows that's his person.

"Where'd you get the rat?" Vonnie asks.

"Walter is a Maltese. He's a teacup."

"Well, I've got a kettle of a snake who could swallow that thing whole. You better keep it on a leash."

"You need to keep your snake in its cage."

Uh-oh. Here we go. She hates when anyone says Lolita belongs in a cage.

"I will not imprison her in her habitat to accommodate your little ankle biter. She was here first. You can keep your dog in a kennel."

"Walter will accompany me on my walks from now on. Dogs need daily walks."

"That thing's legs are two-inches long. Walking around your apartment is plenty of exercise for it."

"Don't call him *it*. His name is Walter."

"You can name it whatever you want. It still needs to be on a leash."

"He will have a proper leash. Unlike some people, I am a responsible pet owner."

"Nobody owns Lolita. She's her own woman."

Autry shakes his head furiously. "Well, if she can get along with Walter, you won't be welcome on our walks."

Walter yips.

"His first bark!" Autry exclaims.

It's hard not to get excited about something that damn cute, but I know Vonnie is taking notes. She'll hold it against anyone who shows this little dog too much affection.

"I don't need you to go on walks. Lollie Girl and I will walk laps around you and your teacup." She turns to go, but she quips over her shoulder, "Walter is a stupid name for a little dog."

"At least I didn't name my pet after a harlot."

Vonnie turns with her eyes narrowed. "You forget I know things about you, little man. You better watch yourself."

He takes a step back, pulling Walter closer as if to protect him. "How dare you?"

"I was born on a dare. And I'll be an unapologetic harlot until the day I die."

"Now, Vonnie, you know I didn't mean—"

"Don't you speak to me right now." She leaves with her head held high, but she goes in a hurry.

"Oh, dear." Autry pets Walter nervously. "That got a little out of hand."

"She'll forgive you," Landry says.

"Not soon enough." Autry sounds genuinely sorry to have upset her. The two of them push each other's buttons all the time. I've never seen either of them back down. I've also never seen Vonnie look truly hurt by his comments or Autry's expression filled with so much regret.

How could such a tiny dog cause so much trouble on his first day here? Walter yips again and we all cheer for him like he just ran a marathon.

Even that hardly puts a smile back on Autry's face, but he gives his new dog head pats and says, "Good boy, Walter."

Landry is on the phone when I come back from lunch, and I hear her say my name before I step into the office. Before she sees me.

"Who is she talking to?" I ask Molly.

She shrugs.

Landry's tone becomes hushed, and her responses clipped.

"Uh-huh," she says. "Exactly."

She smiles at me, but it looks like it's causing her pain. "Oh, definitely."

Her eyes shift away. "Same here."

Spinning her chair so her back is to me now, she says, "Always. That's so funny." For something so funny, she doesn't laugh. "Yeah, absolutely. Thanks again."

She ends the call and immediately opens her emails.

"Who was that?" I ask.

"Oh, that was Tess. She's the office manager at Rough Hands."

"I know his office manager's name. Why were you talking to her?"

"She called about the water bottles he's sponsoring for the pool party. I didn't know if we'd have enough time to still order them, but she says they ship fast. So that's good news."

"Okay. Why were you talking to her about me?"

"We were talking about water bottles."

"And me. I heard you say my name."

Landry sighs. "She's apparently a big fan of the two of you dating. And so am I. It was just a comment, no big deal."

"Don't gossip about me and Dec with Tess. That's weird."

"It's not weird for your friends to talk about you. It wasn't gossip."

Molly chimes in. "Wouldn't you love to be a fly on the wall at Rough Hands? Just to hear what he says to her about you?"

"I can honestly say I've never wished to be a fly. I'm sure she's not all that invested in his love life."

"Oh, she's invested," Landry says.

"What did she say?"

"That he's way less grumpy since y'all got back together. She's convinced you're soulmates."

"You sure were agreeing with her an awful lot."

"Yeah, because I think she's right."

"Soulmates aren't a thing."

"Call it whatever you want."

A tenant comes in to let us know the garage door is stuck open again.

Another walks in right behind him to complain that her vent hood isn't working. The first tenant asks her if she checked to be sure the plug didn't come loose.

"Where does it plug in?" she asks.

"In the cabinet over your stove," he says. "I'll go up with you and take a look if you want."

"Okay. Thanks."

They walk out together. None of us said a word to either of them, but they're leaving much happier than when they walked in. It's not like it was fate, though. Pretty sure no one's destiny hinges on a loose connection.

Declan

"I need to swing by the office real quick." I change lanes without looking over at Rina, assuming she'll be fine with the detour.

"Can't you do that after you drop me off?"

That's what I get for assuming.

"I promised Tess I'd bring you by to meet her the next time I took you to lunch."

"Tess seems very persuasive."

"That's one way to put it." I pull into my parking spot. My name's not on it, but everyone knows not to park here. "You'll like her."

"But we're here to be sure she likes me."

"She already likes you. Come on. I'll lock my office door and show you my big desk."

She ignores my attempt at humor, but she gets out of the truck.

Tess isn't there to greet us. It's quiet. Her music isn't even playing.

"She's probably in the bathroom," I say, looking around and imagining what this space must look like through Rina's eyes. It's a fucking mess. Every flyer and brochure has been taken off the shelves and stacked on the floor. Catalogs are fanned out like they may have been in a stack at some point. "This is probably Tess's project of the day. She likes to spread out while she works."

But she doesn't like silence.

I look down the hall to make sure the bathroom door is closed. If it's open, I'm definitely going to be concerned. The back door bangs and Tess stomps into view. "Whoa, shit, Declan! You scared me. I didn't hear you pull up."

"Where were you?"

"Out back on break. I was on the phone."

"Everything okay?"

"Mom's in the hospital."

"And your sister wants you to come handle everything, right?"

"You guessed it."

"Are you going?"

"I don't want to, but I need a few hours to think about it."

"Okay. Just let me know."

She sees Rina and shakes her head. "Wow. I just made a great first impression, didn't I?"

"Don't worry about it," Rina says. "Families are complicated."

"To say the least. Hi."

"Hi. It's great to meet you. Declan talks about you all the time. All good things."

"Probably not as good as the things he says about you. Thanks for making him easier to be around."

"Hey!" I object.

Tess and Rina laugh. I knew they'd like each other.

"Do you mind if I take off for the rest of the afternoon? I'll cram this stuff back on the shelves."

Tess isn't okay, but I know she doesn't want to say too much in front of someone she doesn't know. Her mom has never been good to her, but her sister has no coping skills, so every time their mom has a crisis, it falls to Tess to sort it out. Her mother has a crisis of some sort every six months. She's consistent in that, if nothing else.

"Take off. I'll put it all back on the shelf. Call me if you need anything."

"Thanks."

She blinks back tears, nods at Carina, and bolts before she starts sobbing.

"I hope her mom's okay." Carina bends down to pick up a stack of flyers. She stacks them neatly on the shelf.

"She'll be fine."

"Does this happen a lot?"

"More often than it should, but it's hard to say no to family, even when they're manipulative and self-destructive."

"At least my mom's just manipulative."

I laugh. "That's not okay either, but you're stronger than Tess in some ways. She looks tough, talks tough, but her heart bleeds easier than she wants people to know. And she tries to take care of the whole damn world."

"She takes care of you pretty well."

"I don't know that I could've gotten this business off the ground without her."

"It's good to have people like that in your life."

"We're all alone now. We don't even have to close my office door for me to show you my big desk."

"You need to take me back to my desk."

"You can't blame me for trying."

Tess steps back inside. "Hey, Carina, I just wanted to tell you I love the candle." She nods at the counter in front of her desk where she's kept it since I gave it to her. "I hope Bathtub Zen takes off for you. It's a cool concept."

Her eyes are red, but she couldn't leave without saying that. That's Tess.

Now Carina looks like she might cry. "Thank you."

Okay, it's time for everybody to leave.

I watch her walk back into The Nouveau, her hair blowing in the wind. Five years apart for no reason at all. For a while after I opened Rough Hands, I'd hope to see her every time I called on a new business. The expectation faded over time, but her memory never did.

When Tess said her name that day, I made her repeat it. She could've said Marina or Gina or Katrina, but she didn't. I'd heard her right.

I'm sure there are hundreds of other women named Carina in Houston, but I knew in my gut I was going to see the right one.

Every day I realize more and more how right this is, and it's taking everything I've got not to rush ahead.

How much longer do I have to keep pretending I'm taking this slow?

Carina

Dropping off products for consignment still makes me nervous. I've got merch in six stores now. Every day, I think this could be a fluke, and they'll all call me to come pick up my stuff because it's not selling.

But today, I got my first electronic payment from an actual brick-and-mortar shop.

And Molly's aunt called to say all my candles in their wine store sold out. She asked me to drop off twice as many to replenish their stock. They've started a waiting list. There are customers waiting to buy my candles. And a check waiting for me.

I've had repeat customers at the farmers market. Bathtub Zen is still a tiny business, but it's a tiny success so far.

Dinner at my parents' house isn't the way I'd like to celebrate tonight, but I promised. It was a compromise, really. Coming to the house for dinner with both of them got me out of another dinner alone with my mother.

Sometimes, my dad is a voice of reason. Other times, he goes right along with her. It's a toss-up, but a better gamble than hoping for her to be reasonable on her own.

The worst part is that I want to tell them about Bathtub Zen, but I know what a bad idea that would be. I called Dec on the way over, and he was super supportive and happy for me. Rough Hands is a legitimately successful business. He owns his building, and a fleet of trucks and equipment, but he still makes me feel like I'm conquering the world.

I walk into the house with my feet barely touching the ground.

My mom takes one look at me and says, "You look flushed. Are you sick?"

"It's warm outside, Mom."

"It'll be summer before we know it."

"Yep."

Dad comes in and hugs me. When we're seated at the table, he says, "So, what's new in your life?"

She's obviously told him I'm seeing Declan again. I suspected this might be an intervention, but I just smile and say, "Nothing much new."

"Nothing?"

"He's not new, Dad. Declan isn't a crewmember for his uncle's landscaping company anymore. He owns his own company, including the building." Real estate investments are my dad's measure of success, no matter what someone does for a living.

"Is that right? Where is it?"

The location meets his approval. "Good choice. There's quick equity to be made in that area if you buy right."

"I don't think he's looking to flip it."

"Equity doesn't have to be cashed out to be valuable. Where does he live?"

"In a van." I spoon broccoli onto my plate. "Down by the river."

"Okay. Message received."

"I don't think it was an unreasonable question," Mom says. "There's nothing wrong with wanting to know where he lives."

"He lives in a house. What's on the chicken?"

Dad answers me. "It's a blend from a spice company we invested in."

"You invested in a spice company?"

"Too sweet, isn't it?" he side-eyes the bite of chicken on his fork.

"Well, don't sound so shocked," Mom says. "We've always supported up-and-coming businesses of various types."

The last thing I'd want in this world is to have my parents as investors in my business. Actually, it's a tie between that and their advice on how to run it. I might never tell them about Bathtub Zen.

With no segue at all, Mom asks if Declan has any children.

"He has five, three boys and two girls, but he has no idea who the mothers are."

To my surprise, my dad actually laughs.

Mom drops her fork. "That's not something to joke about, Carina. I hope you've confirmed if he actually has any kids. You'll find yourself paying some man's child support before you know it."

"Not to brag, but I feel like I might see that one coming, Mom. Doesn't really seem like the kind of thing that would creep up on me."

"I'm just trying to look out for your best interests."

"You always are."

"And what's wrong with that?"

"He doesn't have any kids, but if he did, I'm sure he would exceed his financial obligations. He's not a deadbeat person, so there's no reason to think he'd be a deadbeat dad. New subject, please."

"Is he living with you, Carina? If you're letting that man sponge off you—"

"Why on Earth would you think he was living with me?"

"He was naked in your kitchen!"

"You can't possibly think I move in every man who gets naked in my kitchen. These rolls are good. Did y'all invest in a bakery, too?"

My dad intervenes. "You can't blame your mother for being concerned. She got quite a shock that night."

"He was quite shocked as well when she walked in on him being naked in my kitchen. It's not like he answered the door that way."

"You could've simply said no, he doesn't live there." My father salts his chicken.

"No, he doesn't live there. Can we please find something else to talk about now?"

Ah, the sound of silence.

"Have you been paying attention to the expenses on the pool renovation?"

Her ability to bounce from an unpleasant topic to a worse one is uncanny. "Nope. I've already told you my position on that. Landry's the manager. Her car, her clowns."

"It's only a matter of time before you're the manager there. You may as well start paying closer attention to the budget now."

"What does that mean?"

"You know good and well what it means."

"I'm not taking Landry's job. I may not even stay in property management for much longer."

Fuck. Why did I say that?

"Oh?" My dad sits up. "You have another opportunity in your back pocket?"

"Let me guess," my mom says. "Declan needs a new reception-ist."

"Wow. You're good. It never even occurred to me he might've wormed his way back into my life to steal me away from The Nouveau. What a diabolical plot. I can't believe I almost let him get away with it!"

"Carina, please." Dad rubs his forehead. "What is this alternate career path you're contemplating?"

"I was thinking I might start selling candles and bath bombs. People are shaping careers from cottage industries more and more these days."

My mother's labored exhale is stage-worthy. "You're clearly determined to undermine any attempt at serious conversation tonight."

"I've disclosed Declan's business status, his parental status, his residency status . . . what would be serious enough for you? Do you need to know his blood type? Because I've gotta be honest, I dropped the ball on that one. No idea. I'm bound to end up the subject of a true-crime podcast at this rate."

"You don't think it's at all suspicious that he just showed back up in your life after all this time?"

"My mind boggles at the nefarious possibilities, Mom."

She storms away from the table.

My dad follows her into the kitchen.

I'm not going to sit here like a teenager, waiting for them to come back and announce my punishment for my smart mouth. But I'm not going to sneak out like a teenager either.

As I approach the kitchen, I hear my dad say, "I'm not suggesting she should run out and marry the guy, Angela, but I don't see any way we can dissuade her from their relationship at this point. She's grown. Based on what she's said tonight, he doesn't sound like the worst choice she could make."

Not the worst choice. That's the best he can come up with? Change of plans. I'm absolutely sneaking out. I text Dec from their driveway.

You home?

I can be there in ten minutes.

I'll be there in five.

Challenge accepted.

Declan

WHEN TESS IS HERE, it never seems like this many calls come in, but the damn phone hasn't stopped ringing today. I only lasted two hours on the road before I gave up and came to the office to cover for her. It's impossible to field all the calls while driving.

I'm probably safer here, anyway. It's hard to concentrate in traffic when I can't stop thinking about Rina in my bed the other night after her parents pissed her off at dinner. I'm sorry she can't have a smoother relationship with them, but I'm not sorry she called me to work off her anger.

She wouldn't tell me exactly what happened, but me being back in her life played a part. I gathered that much between rants about her being an adult and them being closed-minded assholes.

Fuck this phone, I swear!

"Rough Hands Landscaping."

I listen to a concerned citizen report one of my drivers for parking on the grass at an office complex where we're building a retaining wall. I've been to the site, and I know exactly where he's parked. I guess she'd prefer he block half the driveway with the trailer.

"I understand your concern, but that grass is all going to be replaced with a native variety after the retaining wall is complete, so—"

She doesn't want to hear a word I have to say. She just wants to be heard.

"Well, he shouldn't have been rude to you. Yes, I'll make sure his boss knows. Thank you for calling. I hope you have a better afternoon."

I hang up before she can start again.

"Rough Hands Landscaping."

Oh, good. Now I get the other side of the story.

"Yeah, she just called. Don't try to defend yourself next time. That never works. Just refer them to building management. I don't have time to talk right now, but you're not in trouble. Get back to work."

"Rough Hands Landscaping."

"Is the owner available?"

"Who's calling?"

"James Adair."

"This is Declan Chillicothe. I'm the owner. What can I do for you?"

"Hello, Declan. I guess my name doesn't mean anything to you, but I'm Carina's dad."

Oh, shit. I forgot she has her mom's last name. He's her biological father, but there's no rhyme or reason to the way they do anything.

"My apology for not recognizing your name, but my question stands, Mr. Adair. What can I do for you?"

"I was wondering if you might have time to meet us for a drink this evening."

"Us?"

"My wife, Angela, and I would like to meet you."

Oh, now you'd like to meet me? What could go wrong?

"I assume since you're bringing your wife, I can bring my girlfriend."

Damn, his silence is louder than his daughter's.

"I'm not sure Carina would have any interest in sitting down with us for a drink right now. And it might be easier to get to know you without her there."

"So, you're asking me to meet with you behind her back?"

"You're welcome to invite her, Declan. I always love seeing my daughter. I'll leave that up to you."

"Where'd you have in mind? Please do me a favor and make it somewhere that I don't have to go home and put on a jacket first."

"H Bar at The Post Oak. It's worth the trouble of a jacket. Six o'clock?"

"Six-thirty."

"We'll be there."

"How'd you know the name of my company?"

"You're one of three landscaping companies in the general area where Carina mentioned you were located, but the tax rolls only list an owner with the first name of Declan for the Rough Hands Landscaping address. Lucky guess."

"Right. See you at six-thirty."

How in the hell do I approach her with this? *Hey, you feel like getting kicked out of H Bar tonight?*

Shit. Why'd I say yes to him? There's no way this doesn't end in a public scene. If she agrees to go with me. Maybe I shouldn't tell her. And then when she finds out, she can stop speaking to all of us.

"Fuck!" I slam my fist on my desk.

"Maybe after lunch?" Rina stands in my office doorway, holding up a bag and looking like a vision. "I wasn't sure you'd be able to get out, so I picked up sandwiches. If you're too busy, I can just drop yours off."

"I'm never too busy for you. I didn't even hear you come in."

"Well, it's probably hard to hear the door when you're beating up your desk."

I forward the phones to voicemail. I'll tell her after we eat. Maybe not right after, but before she leaves.

"I'm starving. Your timing couldn't be better."

She brings me up to date on all the latest tenant drama at The Nouveau. I couldn't do her job, but she's good with people, always sees both sides, and I swear she could calm down a charging boar.

"There must be something in the air. I've had a few crazy calls today."

"Tell me all about them," she says. "It'll help to know I'm not the only one dealing with lunatics this week."

"Hold on to that thought." I start with the woman upset over where my guy parked. That one's funny, and starting with humor can only help, given where this conversation is headed.

"You'd think people would have enough going on in their own lives, but there's always someone who'd rather worry about what other people are doing with theirs."

"On that note, do you want to grab a drink after work?"

"What do nosy people have to do with us having drinks after work?"

"The next call I got was from your dad. He wants to meet for drinks tonight."

"And he wants you to bring me?" She gets up and paces back and forth. "This is just like him to use you to get to me. I can't believe you went along with it!"

"He invited me. Inviting you was my idea. I didn't want you to feel like I was betraying you by meeting him alone."

"Well, could you give me all the information upfront next time? Damn, Dec." She sits back down. "You said yes?"

"I must have because we set a time."

She laughs. "Yeah, he's good at leaving you wondering how or when you agreed to things."

I really hate that I have to tell her the rest.

"Your mom is going to be there, too. I just thought maybe if they got to know me . . ."

"They should get to know you, but that won't happen if I'm there. I'll be defensive, and you'll be defensive on my behalf. It'll be easier for y'all to talk if I'm not there. Besides, you probably have things you'd like to say to them, and you'll hold back in front of me. Promise me you won't hold back. Be yourself and say anything you want."

"You're really not going to go?"

"No."

"Okay. I guess I'm on my own for the inquisition."

"You can handle them, but if you don't want to go, you can cancel."

"No, I can't do that. I said I'd be there. I'll go."

She picks up her purse. "Call me after you get home. If you want to. You don't owe me details or anything."

"I'll call you. Do you have to go already?"

"I do."

"Am I ever going to get to bend you over my desk?"

"Never give up hope." She blows me a kiss. "It's a terrible thing when a dream dies."

"Can I at least get a real kiss?"

"Good luck with my parents."

She leaves me with nothing more than the air kiss. All her reasons for not going make sense, but I'm going to be defensive on her behalf, regardless. I'll always champion her.

Carina

"Was it wrong not to go with him?"

Landry smiles as she lowers her wine glass. "You already know the answer to that."

"I do?"

"It was the right decision. He can handle your parents."

I check the time on my phone. Happy hour isn't over yet, so I know he's still with them, but it's unlikely he's happy about it. "I didn't even ask where they were meeting."

"Do you think there's a chance they might be here?"

"No, I can't see my dad sipping scotch under a neon sign urging him not to do cocaine in the bathroom."

"Good. Then you're in a safe space. Relax."

Our cheese board arrives, and we place our dinner orders. I wish my mother could hear us openly asking the server if our coupon code is still good. The only thing that would embarrass her more is the glee on my face when he says yes.

Dec won't use coupons either. But that's all he has in common with my parents, and I doubt that's come up over drinks.

I wonder what they're talking about. Are they prying into his finances? Rhetorical question, of course. They're definitely doing that, but in the sneakiest ways possible, I'm sure. Dec's smart. And guarded about his private information. He won't tell them anything he doesn't want them to know. But they'll try.

What are they saying about me? How I refuse to live up to my potential? I didn't tell him they don't know about Bathtub Zen. Oh, well. It's too late to ask him not to mention it. I could text him, but he probably won't look at his phone until he's in his truck.

Our BOGO dinner specials are delicious. We're debating if we should get dessert when my phone buzzes.

I survived.

Finishing up dinner with Landry. Wanna come over?

Meet me at my office.

"Definitely skipping dessert. I think I'm about to be bent over a desk."

He steps out of his truck when I pull in next to him.

"Why'd you wait out here?"

"So you didn't have to get out of your car and walk in alone."

"I would've been fine."

"This way I know for sure." He takes my hand and leads me into the building. Without turning on the lights, he pins me to the wall and kisses me.

"How bad was it?" I ask.

"It was exactly what I expected. I'm not defending them, but you know they act that way because they love you and don't know how else to show it, right?" He brushes my hair away from my eyes.

"Yeah, I know, but that doesn't excuse their bad behavior."

"You're absolutely right. It doesn't. But you should always know when someone loves you, even when they fall short of what you deserve." There is a security light shining outside the front window. We are standing in the glowing cone it casts on the wall. Spotlighted. I can see his eyes holding on to mine. "I love you, Rina. I love you enough to have drinks with your parents every week for the rest of my life. I promise I'll keep working to show you, but I need to be able to tell you, too."

"I dreamed you said it a few weeks ago."

"You weren't dreaming. I was just too scared to say it when you were awake."

"Were you only scared to say it or scared to love me?"

"Maybe a little of both. But I'm over it. I love you. Fearlessly."

"I love you, too. Fearlessly."

"I hear a desk calling your name."

"Let's go see what it wants."

As soon as we're in his office, I plant my palms on his desk and wait for him to take over.

His hands fist the sides of my skirt and pull it up over my hips. He lowers my panties to my ankles, and then yanks to signify he wants me to step out of them.

Twisting my satin thong into a figure eight once, twice, three times, he says, "Give me your wrists."

We both know the symbolic cuffs wouldn't hold me if I wanted to escape them, but I don't. His desktop is cool under my cheek. My shoulders lie flat against it, too, and my lower back pushes my hips higher to ensure his access to my pussy.

I bite my bottom lip when he slaps my ass, and my arms extend long behind my back. The stretch releases tension from my shoulders to the base of my spine, and then I relax and enjoy the sting of his hand when he strikes the next blow.

When his fingers glide down to enjoy how wet I am for him, we groan in unison. The edge of his desk digs into my hipbones with the initial thrust of his stiff cock, but the pain recedes into the shadows, replaced by pleasure and an immeasurable craving for more.

More of this. More of us. More, so much more . . .

Declan

"Have I told you how glad I am to have you back?"

"Only a dozen times." Tess tosses the plush river otter I gave her this morning up and catches it. "But what I need is for you to take those water bottles to The Nouveau. They were supposed to be shipped straight to them. Their pool party is this weekend, Dec."

I grab the otter when she tosses him up again. "I'm glad your mom is okay, too."

"Thanks," she says. "For now, anyway."

"It's okay to be glad for now. Nobody can control the future." I hand the otter to her.

"I know. Go deliver those bottles. Get out of here so I can get some work done."

My back has improved enough that Dorian says I can switch to monthly adjustments now. I'm happy to have less back pain, but as much as I hated coming here to begin with, it's become part of my routine, and I hate having my routine interrupted.

Rina will laugh when I tell her about this development. I can already hear her telling me it's good to break up routines. Knowing she's right doesn't make me like it any better.

Autry greets me when I arrive at The Nouveau. They should make him the honorary doorman. "I heard you got a dog, but I didn't know he'd be so ferocious."

"Don't underestimate Walter," he says.

"That's right," Vonnie says as she comes up the sidewalk behind me. "He's a little terror."

I'll never get used to the sight of her wearing that snake around, but the dog appears happy to see them both. I step aside to let her walk in ahead of me. The snake is entirely uninterested in the panting little fluff ball, but Vonnie rubs his ears and kisses the top of his head. This place is the motherland of unlikely scenarios.

Landry is excited to see the boxes in my arms.

"I've got more in the truck."

The younger maintenance guy, Holden, walks by, and Carina yells his name. "Can you bring in some boxes from Declan's truck?"

"Sure. Is it locked?"

"Yeah." I toss him the keys. "It's the black Ford."

"Got it."

When he's out the door, she says, "You showed up at the perfect time. We need Vonnie and Autry to sign this card for him."

"Is it his birthday?"

"He's graduating from college," Landry says. "We haven't told him yet, but we're making the pool reopening his graduation party, too."

Vonnie and Autry excitedly scribble their signatures on the card and walk out together. Molly hides the card in her desk like she's been trusted with something priceless.

"These came out great." Landry holds up one of the water bottles for further inspection, and Carina and Molly echo her approval.

Vaughn comes in to ask Landry if she's done for the day.

"Almost. Carina and I need to go over some final plans for the party."

"I guess that answers my next question, too," I say.

"Well," Vaughn says, "since we're both being shunned, you want to go up to the roof and drink a beer?"

"Sure."

Holden sets two more boxes on the floor. Vaughn invites him to come up and join us, but he says he's going to take off after he brings in the rest of the boxes. Molly offers to help him, and

I'm pretty sure there's more behind the smile he flashes than just gratitude for her help with boxes.

There's got to be something in the water.

Carina

Landry has declared that the final episode of *The Rest of the Story* calls for a specialty cocktail and pizza. "When the stakes get this high, you need heartier food and drinks. I don't make the rules."

I'm up for whatever food she wants as long as we can get it here quickly. I worked at the farmers market today, and I didn't even have time to grab a snack. The last thing I ate was an apple while Dec loaded boxes into my car this morning.

He lent his charms to my table again. I think he enjoys working at the farmers market almost as much as I do. We make a good team.

Never dreamed I'd see Declan Chillicothe selling bubble bath, but he works that shit like nobody's business. Every time women stopped to read the new slogans on the bath products to each other and giggled, especially the one that says *Okay, But You Gotta Get Me Wet First,* he got a little uncomfortable. He tried to hide it, but I saw it. It was cute. He caught me smiling about it a few times. His dismissive smirk was cute, too.

Landry's calling our drink for the final episode a cliffhanger, which this episode is bound to be. "I looked up a recipe for a drink called a cliffhanger, but there were lots of different ones, and none of them sounded especially good, so I created my own."

It's just lemonade with vanilla vodka and cherries, but she put it in the blender with a splash of coconut cream to make it pink and frothy. I hold it up to the light. "It looks like there's been a shark feeding frenzy in my glass."

"Ooh, I like that. Let's call it a shark frenzy instead of a cliffhanger. It's more fun."

"As shark attacks are so often described."

It's no surprise the three remaining authors' stories are accepted for the anthology. That was part of the premise from the start, but when they find out the three who left the cabin are also being included, the diva crowns activate.

And when they find out all the contributing authors are being listed on the cover in alphabetical order, Kissing in the Rain goes ballistic. "My last name starts with W! Will our names be printed in a larger font?"

The publisher, Madelyn Woodvale rolls her eyes. "No, they will not. You do remember this is for charity, right?"

"It's not fair."

"As someone whose last name also begins with a W, I commiserate. Alphabetical listings are not to our advantage." She pours herself another cup of tea as if the matter has been sorted.

Trademarked Eyes is happy because her last name starts with an A, but she also feels their names should appear in a larger font.

Lars Bennington interrupts before the third author can raise her own concerns. "Shall we tell them?"

Madelyn nods.

"We have news," Lars begins. "News I think you're going to love." He steeples his fingers under his chin and shifts his eyes side-to-side as if he's deciding whether to let them in on said news.

When no one takes the bait and begs him to go on, he drops his hands and says, "You're going on tour to promote the anthology. And there will be a specialty tie-in cover for the show. With your picture on it."

"Only the three of us?" Trademarked Eyes asks.

"The cover will feature all six authors contracted for the show." Madelyn sets her teacup on the table. "There will be a group photoshoot this afternoon."

"They're coming back here?" Kissing in the Rain is livid. "Today?"

Lars squares his shoulders. "They're not only coming here for the photoshoot. They'll be joining you on the tour."

"Fuck that! I'm calling my agent!" Diva Number Three races for the stairs. She stumbles halfway up and falls. The camera captures her grasping for the handrail as she tumbles down a few steps, her face horror-stricken. They replay it in slow motion. Twice.

There is a montage scene of the other three authors arriving at the cabin for the group photo. It shifts to the six of them in position on the front steps, makeup sparkling, hair blown by fans as if a dramatic wind is sweeping over them, and then someone screams, the camera topples, and a promo for the book tour precedes the credits.

"I'm not sure I care about watching season two with the tour," Landry says.

I toss my pizza crust into the box. "I bet everyone is saying that right now, but they'll do a reunion show to hype it, and we'll all be right back in."

"I hate how true that is." She holds up her empty glass. "More shark frenzy?"

"It's already in the blender. It would be a shame to let it go to waste."

"Do you think those authors are all friends off-camera?"

"Probably for short periods of time," I say. "I'm not sure any of them are long-term people."

"I think anyone can form a lasting bond under the right circumstances."

My head feels like it's hosting a shark frenzy when my alarm goes off. Landry and I both have to be up early this morning. She and Vaughn are picking up the food and drinks for the pool party.

I've got to drop off more products and collect a couple of checks. I'll be back later to help set up. Declan is coming to the party. He's not just a vendor, he's a sponsor, though he doesn't want any attention for that.

Landry will make a big announcement, anyway, just like she's going to make sure everyone knows Holden is getting his degree and leaving us to go be a big deal screenwriter.

Holden has invited a few friends, but he insists we can't call it his graduation party because he's afraid it might bother the residents. We've tried to tell him they'll all be happy to celebrate with him.

I think he's uncomfortable in the limelight. He better get used to it. He's going into a field where self-promotion is mandatory. It's hard at first, but he'll adjust. If I can do it, anyone can.

Vaughn comes across the hall to make sure Landry is up and getting ready. He's former military, and sometimes it shows. She's annoyed that he's here to keep her on schedule when she wants to sleep for another thirty minutes, but he's brought breakfast tacos, so he's a hero in my book.

I help myself to a few Advil from her medicine cabinet and leave the lovebirds to their power struggle, taking a taco to go.

The weather is beautiful. Perfect day to reopen the pool.

I actually get to witness the sale of one of my candles at the first shop I stop at. It's the most amazing feeling, but I stand back and pretend to be browsing. After the customer has left, I introduce myself to the sales clerk and tell her I have some products to restock.

She excitedly tells me how much she loves my labels. Amazing moment number two. And then she gives me the check the owner left for me in the register. Amazing moment number three.

This day is almost too perfect. I shake away the feeling, trying to shed my skepticism. When things go too smoothly, I automatically expect trouble. I'm trying to let that shit go. On year three and counting.

There's no line at the drive-through when I pull in for coffee on my way to the next store. I get a free pastry sample at the window. Better and better.

I catch every green light for the rest of my drive, and a car pulls out of a spot right in front of the door, giving me rockstar parking. *Yes!*

When I approach the store with the large box in my arms, a customer holds the door open for me. People can be so great.

"Carina? What is that?"

That's unmistakably my mother's voice, but the scene is so improbable, I nearly drop the box. My eyes focus on the woman holding the door as my brain tries to reconcile my mother committing a random act of kindness. I've literally watched her let the go in the faces of dozens of people.

She doesn't do it to be intentionally inconsiderate; she just doesn't even realize they're there.

It's actually her. She pushes the door wider so I can finagle the box through the opening. I walk to the counter and she follows, hot on my heels.

"Carina!" The owner comes around to give me a side hug and helps me put the box on the counter. "I can't wait to see what you brought. I've cleared a bigger table for you."

"Why do you have a table?" my mother asks. "What's in the box?"

"I told you at dinner. I'm selling candles and bath bombs."

"You said that in jest."

I open the box and pull out the first thing my hand lands on. Oh, good. It's the candle with the word pussy on the label.

"Carina Elizabeth!"

"It's funny, Mom. People like to laugh."

The store owner comes to my defense. "I wasn't sure how my customers would react, but I laughed so hard when I saw her labels that I had to give her products a shot. They're a hit. We're nearly sold out."

"This is a thing you're actually doing. It's your job?"

"For now, it's a side hustle. But it might be my job one day."

"You want to open your own shop selling candles with dirty words on them?"

"Maybe. Someday. I don't know. Right now, I just want to keep doing what I'm doing."

My mother peers into the box to see what other scandalous merchandise I've schlepped in from my trunk.

"I was going to send your payment electronically," the owner says, "but you were on your way to open a new business bank account the last time you were here, and I didn't want to send it to the wrong place."

"Oh, it's already linked. It won't change anything on your end."

"Perfect. I'll send it now."

My mother pulls her head out of the box. "You have a business bank account?"

"Yes."

"Are you incorporated?"

"Not quite there yet."

"Have you spoken to a CPA? I'm sure Niles would be happy to sit down and—"

"I'm using Declan's CPA."

"Okay. It never hurts to get a second opinion."

"It's a sole proprietorship, not a cancer diagnosis."

She looks at the candle label again. "Your name isn't on it."

"You're welcome."

"What's wrong with Carina's Candles? I gave you such a beautiful name. I don't see why you wouldn't use it."

I carry the box from the counter to my new table. It's significantly more space. There might be room to bring in another box. "I sell more than candles, Mom." I hand her a four-pack of my double-sized bath bombs. The label says *Biggo Bath Bombs: Because Of Course Size Matters!*

Did she actually laugh at that? Huh.

"You came up with all these jokes on your own?"

"They're all mine."

"And you're making money?"

"A profit even."

"Well, a profitable hobby is better than one that loses money, I guess."

I tell myself she meant that as a compliment.

"Here, you need this more than I do." She slips a tube of something from her shopping bag into my purse. "With those dark circles under your eyes, people would think I was the daughter. Get some rest when you're done here."

Ah, there she is.

She pats my arm and wishes me luck. I'm not sure if she means it for sales or my raccoon eyes.

Wait. Where'd that bag of bath bombs go? She took them?

That's a thousand times better than the compliment she attempted. She wouldn't have taken them if she didn't want them.

Angela Melendez is going to use my bath bombs.

My phone dings with the notification that a payment just hit my account.

Declan

ATTENDING A CLIENT'S POOL party is the type of event I'd normally do anything to get out of, but The Nouveau is a different story.

Carina's tossing beach balls into the pool when I arrive. "These light up!" she yells when I come through the gate. "I can't wait for it to get dark."

She's had a good day. I spent thirty minutes on the phone earlier listening to her happily tell me all about it. When she dropped the news that she ran into her mom while she was restocking, her tone didn't even change.

Vaughn is taping down the extension cord for the deejay.

"Anything I can do to help?" I ask.

He shakes his head and laughs. "Not unless you can come up with a valid reason for me to get out of this party."

"If I was that smart, I'd have gotten myself out of it."

As soon as the gate officially opens, the music starts, and the party is on.

Despite the No Pets Allowed sign, Vonnie shows up wearing her snake. And a bikini. Autry has left his little dog in his apartment, but he's right by Vonnie's side, offering her his sweater, which she swats away. He protests. She tunes him out and walks to the table where Landry is handing out party favors, returning with a lei around her neck and one for Autry. He grumbles the whole time she's putting it on him.

I find a post I can lean against to get out of the way of flying beach balls. It's a perfect spot to avoid most of the partyers but still be able to watch Carina interact with them. Her ability to connect with people impresses me. I'm good with small talk and sales pitches, but she can engage in meaningful conversations with anyone.

The deejay introduces Landry to draw the first round of raffle winners. Before she hands the mic back to him, she announces the sponsors for the party. Somehow, I've gained platinum sponsor status with cheap, refillable water bottles. I'm grateful when she moves on to announcing Holden's news. His achievement is a lot more noteworthy than my contribution.

When the party finally ends at ten o'clock, people scramble to grab a glowing beach ball. The things that excite people will never cease to amaze me.

I stick around to help with clean-up, and then I follow Carina home. The best part of the night is yet to come, even if she falls asleep as soon as we crawl into her bed. I'll still get to wake up next to her.

Carina

I ROLL OVER AND stare at Declan, willing him to wake up. It works.

"Why are you watching me sleep?"

"You're not asleep."

"I was until you woke me up with your penetrating stare."

"Nobody is getting penetrated this morning." I laugh at my joke. He reopens one eye. "We've got to get up for yoga."

"We're skipping it."

"Oh, no we're not. Come on. You'll be wide awake and energized after the class."

"I could get that same feeling from more sleep." His arm comes down heavy on my waist, and he attempts to pull me closer.

I wriggle free and hop out of bed. He watches me get dressed. "Are you making coffee?"

"No. I'll puke if I drink coffee before yoga. Coffee is my reward for after."

"I won't puke if I drink it before class."

"Then you should get up and make yourself some. I'm going to brush my teeth."

His groan makes me laugh. So much protesting for something we both know he's going to do.

"Ahhh," I savor the first sip of my well-earned latte. "Aren't you glad we got up and went to yoga?"

"I'm glad it's over. You tricked me into that class. I thought it was going to be regular yoga."

"The dread beforehand and the gratitude after are two of the best parts. And Ashtanga is a regular form of yoga."

My mother's number lights up my phone screen. "Speaking of dread."

Dec reaches over and taps my screen to answer the call. He shrugs. "You shouldn't have tricked me."

"Hi, Mom."

"I have news that's going to make you very happy."

"You've decided to put me up for adoption?"

"What?"

"What?"

"Do you want to hear this news or not?"

"Yes. I'm sorry. What is your happy news?"

"I've found you the perfect location."

"What are you talking about? Perfect location for what?"

"Your store."

"I'm nowhere near being ready to open a store."

"Well, get ready because we bought it."

"We?"

"Yes, your father and I are buying it, and you can do a lease to purchase from us. It's the cutest little house. Commercially zoned. Decent parking. It's an insurance agency now, but their lease is up at the end of the month."

"Renew the insurance agent's lease."

"Oh, don't be stubborn. This is a fantastic opportunity."

"When and if I decide to open a store, I will choose the location. I will decide whether to lease or buy. I will decide how cute it should be and how many fucking parking spaces it needs! I will make *all* the decisions because Bathtub Zen is mine!"

"You're obviously having a bad morning. We'll discuss this later."

"Actually, I am having a great morning! And we are never discussing this again! Goodbye."

Dec flinches. "I am so sorry."

"It's fine. It wouldn't have been nearly as satisfying to yell at her voicemail." I laugh.

And then I laugh harder.

And then I realize I can't stop laughing.

"Holy shit. I've never felt a greater release in my life," I finally manage to say. "I can't believe how many endorphins that unleashed. Damn. I feel like an escaped hostage. And I don't even have to run for my life."

"Do you think they really bought the building?"

"Oh, they definitely did. My mother is a mood investor. She buys property the way some women buy shoes. Fortunately for her, she has good instincts."

"When we get to your apartment, I'll try to give you the second greatest release of your life."

"This is the best weekend ever."

Dec suggests we shower together. I'd already assumed that was happening.

He doesn't bitch that I've made the water too hot or anything. My loofah looks small in his hand as he rubs circles over my body. The steam is infused with notes of tonka bean and citrus from my favorite body wash. I couldn't recreate this scent if I tried, but I know I'll be able to call up this memory and smell it anytime I want for the rest of my life.

His eyes follow the foamy suds he's creating on my skin. When he sees me watching, he drops the loofah and pushes my back against the tiles.

"I've had a few lucky breaks," he says. "Things that went my way to get me where I am, and I worked hard to make the most of them, but I'll work harder for you. Always."

"You don't have to keep proving yourself to me."

"I'll never stop."

His kiss consumes me.

A second chance at us is the most golden opportunity I've ever been offered. And I was raised to recognize a good deal when I see one.

"Shower sex is overrated," I say when his hard-on stabs me in the abdomen.

"Are you telling me I have to carry you all the way to your bed to fuck you?"

"The rugs in here are really soft."

I never knew I could feel so adored on a bathroom floor.

The buzz of an incoming text wakes me up. I have to push Dec's arm off mine to reach for my phone. It's a picture from Landry.

My squeal wakes him from a sound sleep. "What? What is it?" He sits up before his eyes are fully opened. He's disoriented, but ready to fight a bear.

"They're engaged!"

"Who?"

"Landry and Vaughn. I can't believe she said yes. Look at her hand!"

He rubs his eyes and squints at the photo. "The way you screamed, I thought somebody was in the apartment."

I kiss his shoulder. "There is someone in my apartment."

A smile replaces his agitated expression. "If you want to congratulate her, you better do it quick because I'm about to punish you for waking me up like that."

I've never typed so fast in my life. The moment my phone leaves my hand, he yanks me to the center of the bed. "Roll over so I can leave my handprint on your perfect ass."

"It already burns from Ashtanga."

"That's in your muscles. I'm going to make your pretty skin sting."

"After the things I let you do to me on my bathroom floor?" I roll slowly onto my stomach.

"Remind me to get the wedges the next time we attempt any of that on the floor." His rough hand massages my sore glutes. I moan and sink into the mattress.

"Oh, you're not going back to sleep, not after you woke me up."

"Then you better keep me awake."

The first stinging slap is followed by more massaging, and then neck kisses that make me squirm against the sheet. He rolls on top of me and swipes my hair out of the way to plant kisses over more of my neck.

"If this is your idea of punishment, please punish me more."

"You're not calling the shots here."

"Put your dick inside me." I push my hips up. "Hmm, interesting."

"I was going to do that, anyway."

We both laugh as he thrusts deeper. "You want more?"

"I want it all."

"Take it."

I slide back. He pushes forward.

The give and take of a perfect partnership.

Declan

Two Years Later . . .

RINA PUSHES A TABLE two feet to the left. "There. That's perfect."

I drop a rug onto the floor and use the toe of my boot to unroll it.

"That goes upstairs," she says.

"I thought this one was for the store."

"No, it's for our bedroom."

"You couldn't have mentioned that before we put the bed to-gether?"

"It doesn't go under the bed. It goes next to it." She walks over and leans into my chest. "If anyone had told me two years ago that I'd be working in a multi-use property, this is not what I would've envisioned."

"Do you think you're going to miss property management?"

"Not at all. You sure you're okay with living above my store?"

"Our loft upstairs is bigger than my house was. Closer to my office. It's perfect."

"I still can't believe what a steal we got on this place."

"Thanks to your parents."

"All they did was find it. We got it on our own. And we put in all the sweat equity to transform it."

"We got a lucky break, and we made the most of it."

"It's what we do."

She pulls away from me to move the table back to its original position. I know she'll move it a dozen more times before she makes a final decision.

I roll the rug back up and carry it up the stairs. I'm sure I put it on the wrong side of the bed, but rearranging things is her favorite activity right now.

Standing at the bedroom window, I look down on our small backyard. It's big enough for a greenhouse and a deck with a hot tub. I've picked out every tropical bush and flower, the new fencing materials, and the rocks for the water feature.

I'm itching to get out there and bring my vision to life, but Bathtub Zen opens in less than two weeks. We have to get the store ready first. Then I can focus on the exterior spaces, and she can start adding new projects for me to tackle in our living space. She says it's done, but I know better. Our weekends have been devoted to this place for the past eight months, and I don't see that ending immediately.

The living room, dining area, and kitchen are open-concept, and from the vantage point of our bedroom door, the area looks huge. It's the biggest place I've ever lived, that's for sure. The guest bedroom is nearly as big as the primary. She grew up with large rooms. I'm still getting used to them.

I hear voices downstairs. Half the store is for consignment merchandise. People have been dropping off boxes all day. But when I hear the beeping of a truck backing up, I know the sign is here.

My feet take the stairs two at a time. Rina designed the sign, and I want to see her face when she sees it for the first time.

She's standing on the wide front porch waiting for it to be lifted into place. I drape my arm across her shoulder. We're surrounded by sleek, minimalist signs. She worried that going with a retro neon vibe would be too out of place for the street, but as it rises to the top of the pole, it's the only choice I can imagine for Bathtub Zen.

"Is it too much?" she asks, biting her bottom lip.

"It's going to stand out in the most perfect way possible."

The owner of the hair salon across the street yells, "I love your sign!"

A car slows and the passenger window lowers. "Are you open?"

"We open on the sixteenth!" Carina shouts.

"We'll be back!"

Landry and Vaughn walk up the sidewalk, and she raises the bottle in her hand. "I brought cheap champagne to toast to your terribly tacky sign!" No one encouraged Carina to trust her gut on this neon sign more than Landry. She stops and snaps a few pics of it going up. Then she turns her phone toward us.

She doesn't have to tell us to smile. We couldn't stop if we tried.

I hope you enjoyed being a fly on the wall at The Nouveau and all the other places Carina and Declan showed you. Most of all, I hope you fell in love with them falling back in love. And I hope you'll want to read more from me. Thank you for spending your precious time in my pages.

Steamy Rom-Com Duologies

VENGEFUL VIXENS:

Your Boss Says Hi!

She's only looking for a rebound guy, but her ex's boss plays for keeps. He's a former NFL player who used to have thousands of women screaming his name every week. Now, he only wants one woman to scream his name, and she just might become his biggest fan yet.

https://books2read.com/VengefulVixens1

Your Trainer Says Hi!

She only wants to see her ex's beloved personal trainer in the gym—until he convinces her his hot tub could do wonders for her aching muscles. He isn't wrong, but between the heat, the bubbles, and his off-the-clock skills, she might be in too deep before she knows it. He's definitely not her type. So why can't she stop seeing him?

https://books2read.com/VengefulVixens2

NAUGHTY AT THE NOUVEAU:
Maintenance & Management

She's the new property manager. He's the new maintenance supervisor. They rub each other the wrong way . . . until they start to rub each other so very right. There's a non-fraternization policy, so they really shouldn't. But there's only one bed!

https://books2read.com/NaughtyAtTheNouveau1

Landscaping & Leasing

The book you just read!

Small Town Second Chance Romance

Peri

They were the wildest couple in town once, but that was a long time ago. They're not restless small-town kids anymore. And she's not back in town to see him. But seeing him once won't hurt anything. How much trouble could they get into as adults? Hardly any if you disregard the dirty karaoke and the lewd (allegedly) graffiti . . . and that old flame reigniting like an inferno.

https://books2read.com/Peri